HE SAW IT

"Go get the sheriff,"

"Friend, you're crazy, moving.

Later, much later, Clint would wonder if the whole thing wouldn't have turned out differently if DeGraw had listened to him.

The shotgun rider jumped down from the stage, leaving the ten-gauge in the boot. The moment he hit the ground, all hell broke loose.

The first shot came from Clint's side of the street. It caught the shotgun rider dead center in his chest, spinning him slightly and sending his body back toward the stage's wheels . . .

DON'T MISS THESE
ALL-ACTION WESTERN SERIES
FROM THE BERKLEY PUBLISHING GROUP

THE GUNSMITH by *J. R. Roberts*
Clint Adams was a legend among lawmen, outlaws, and ladies. They called him . . . the Gunsmith.

LONGARM by *Tabor Evans*
The popular long-running series about U.S. Deputy Marshal Long—his life, his loves, his fight for justice.

SLOCUM by *Jake Logan*
Today's longest-running action Western. John Slocum rides a deadly trail of hot blood and cold steel.

BUSHWHACKERS by *B. J. Lanagan*
An all-new series by the creators of Longarm! The rousing adventures of the most brutal gang of cutthroats ever assembled—Quantrill's Raiders.

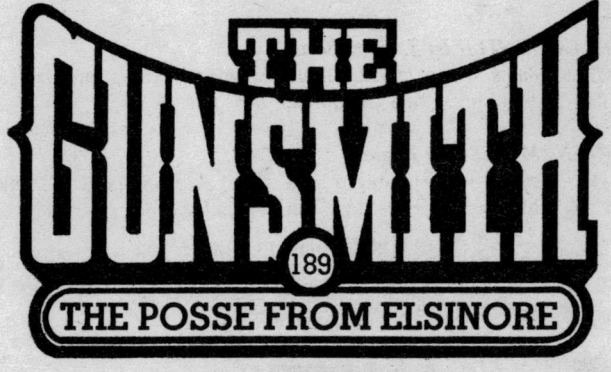

THE POSSE FROM ELSINORE

J. R. ROBERTS

JOVE BOOKS, NEW YORK

If you purchased this book without a cover, you should be aware that this book is stolen property. It was reported as "unsold and destroyed" to the publisher, and neither the author nor the publisher has received any payment for this "stripped book."

THE POSSE FROM ELSINORE

A Jove Book / published by arrangement with
the author

PRINTING HISTORY
Jove edition / September 1997

All rights reserved.
Copyright © 1997 by Robert J. Randisi.
This book may not be reproduced in whole
or in part, by mimeograph or any other means,
without permission. For information address:
The Berkley Publishing Group, 200 Madison Avenue,
New York, New York 10016, a member of Penguin Putnam Inc.

The Putnam Berkley World Wide Web site address is
http://www.berkley.com

ISBN: 0-515-12145-2

A JOVE BOOK®
Jove Books are published by The Berkley Publishing Group,
200 Madison Avenue, New York, New York 10016, a member of
Penguin Putnam Inc.
JOVE and the "J" design are trademarks
belonging to Jove Publications, Inc.

PRINTED IN THE UNITED STATES OF AMERICA

10 9 8 7 6 5 4 3 2 1

ONE

The pretty little claybank died a good dozen miles outside of town. The sun was not even above the tops of the pines and a crisp morning chill still hung in the air when she moaned softly and rolled into the dirt.

Clint Adams had been riding two, maybe three hours from where he broke camp. The horse collapsed on a level trail, her heart already quiet before she was all the way on the ground. Bad heart, was what he thought, but there was no way of knowing for sure. No way of knowing and no need to know. All that was important was that she was dead. And he could be damned sure of that.

Clint looked down at the poor beast, her eyes rolled back in her head, and said, "Shit."

He'd purchased the claybank in San Francisco for the long ride back to Labyrinth, Texas. This trip out, he'd taken a train to San Francisco, leaving Duke, his big black gelding, home for once. Now he regretted the decision.

It was thirty miles back to the last town. Ahead lay Elsinore, Nevada. Clint stood there a spell, studying the animal and feeling the pull of both towns. The hundred dollars he had, fifty in his pocket and another fifty secreted in his saddle, told him to move forward to Elsinore and whatever pleasures and opportunities for work it offered.

Shouldering his saddle and bedroll, and hoisting the rifle in his left hand, he began walking. It took the better part of six miles before he quit thinking of the beast he'd left on the trail. After that, he thought of the town. There would be hot baths, smooth whiskey, clean beds with cool sheets, and, of course, women. Walking, he began putting them in order of which he would take first. Each, after all, had its own advantages and pleasures. The trick was deciding how to mix them.

Before he could come to any firm conclusions, the town appeared beyond an unexpected turn in the trail. It lay down a smooth slope of a hill, laid out like on a map. From a distance, it wasn't much to look at. Eight or nine solid buildings of wood and perhaps double that many tents and lean-tos. It was what he expected of the Nevada mining town that had seen better days. Although never an outright boomtown, the place had managed to hang on, its life secure at the end of a Southern Pacific railhead, known for its square dealings.

Clint walked slowly down the center of the town,

savoring the sidelong glances from the four or five citizens who happened to be on the boards. They were not the unpleasant, probing stares he had encountered in other towns, but rather just curious glances at this horseless stranger. He returned the glances with a pleasant nod and kept moving, passing the Wells Fargo office, the sheriff's office and jail, and then the livery. He kept moving to the center of the town and the hotel.

The hotel, the Elsinore Palace, wasn't much of a palace, but it was the best lodgings he'd seen in a spell. Two floors of weathered wood and a faded sign that announced the name. Both paying shabby tribute to days long gone and not likely to return.

Clint pushed through the batwing doors into the cool dusty dark of the lobby. A couple of loafers sat in the dark corner, far back from any stray light that the dusty windows might let in. Their murmuring stopped at the sight of Clint, and the shabby lobby fell into silence.

Yet, for all its shabbiness, the front desk affected an air of luxury with its marble top and gleaming brass bell.

The manager, a fat man with a thin mustache, stood behind the desk, polishing the bell. When Clint entered, he didn't cease in his task, rather he switched hands and raised his head. "Howdy," he said, and kept polishing.

Clint set his load down before the desk and nodded. "I'll need a room and a hot bath," he said.

"Yes, sir," the manager answered, then ceased his work on the bell. "That be two dollar for the room, fifty cent for the bath. In advance. Hotel policy.'' He seemed a little shy at saying this last bit, perhaps judging that a bit of trail dust might make whatever money this tall stranger had vanish. Perhaps even making the likelihood of any more less certain.

"That's fine," Clint said, bringing a twenty-dollar gold piece from his pocket. "That a saloon I saw down the boards?"

The manager brightened at the sight of the money and quickly grabbed it up off the counter. A moment later he'd made a small stack of greenbacks appear from under the marble counter. "Yes, sir," the manager said, abandoning the pile of money before Clint. "Finest saloon in town."

"It wouldn't be the only saloon in town now, would it?"

"That too, sir," the manager said, smiling. "I can have the boy bring your things up to the room, then fetch you when the bath is ready."

"Do that then," Clint answered, pocketing the paper money.

This was the moment the manager had been waiting for; with some flourish, he reached out and tapped the bell's plunger twice in rapid succession with the palm of his hand.

Clint waited for something to happen. When nothing happened immediately, the manager tapped the bell again, twice.

"I heard you the first time, you damned fool," a voice said from behind the manager. Then a door opened and Clint saw an old man, stooped and grizzled, come through the door.

THE POSSE FROM ELSINORE

"Take this gentleman's belongings up to room four," the manager said briskly.

The old man looked at the saddle, bedroll, and rifle, weighing them mentally for a few moments before making a move, then grabbed them up and turned his back on Clint and the manager as he headed up the stairs.

"He'll fetch you when the bath is ready," the manager said, smiling.

"That's fine, then," Clint said, turning toward the door and the street.

"Another fifty cent, I can have him air out that roll, brush your clothes," the manager called hopefully.

"Let's see about that bath first," Clint answered, not turning.

Pushing through the doors to the street, he heard the low murmur of the loafers and manager start up again.

The bar dog behind the polished length of the bar looked so much like the hotel manager that Clint thought maybe the fat rascal had snuck himself out the back door of the hotel and raced to enter the second establishment to take up position behind the polished mahogany and clean that as he had the brass bell.

"What'll it be, friend?" the bar dog asked, leaving off his polishing to lean palms down on the bar.

"Whiskey," Clint answered, peeling off the largest of the paper money and placing it on the bar. "That enough for a bottle?"

The barkeep poured the first drink into a glass that

might have been washed once, maybe, in more prosperous times, then nodded. "That'll do."

Clint watched the money vanish, then took a drink. With the first taste of the whiskey he began to feel better. The familiar warmth sliding into him, down into his belly, left him wanting another.

"You come a long ways, friend?" the barkeep asked.

"Long enough," Clint answered, sipping now at his third drink.

"Coming down from the north or from the east?"

"Up, came in from the south," Clint answered.

"San Francisco?"

"That's right."

"There's a town."

"It's quite a town."

"Pardon my asking, I didn't see you ride in," the barkeep said, leaning in close now. "Stage ain't in till tomorrow. Train, not till the end of the week."

"My horse gave out on me about twelve miles out," Clint answered, finishing off what was in his glass and pouring another.

"Lame?"

"Dead," Clint said, taking a smooth, slow sip from the welcome drink. "She gave out on me on the trail. Pretty little thing."

"Bad piece of luck, that," the barkeep said. "But they'll do that sometimes."

They stood in silence then for a full ten minutes, Clint sipping at his whiskey, the bar dog nodding. Finally he said, "Damned bad piece of luck, 'bout that horse."

THE POSSE FROM ELSINORE 7

Then they stood in silence some more, until another customer came in.

The barkeep excused himself and moved down to the end of the bar to serve the new customer. "What'll it be, friend?" he asked.

Clint studied the new customer. He was a tall man with red hair and a red beard. Probably not more than thirty-five, he wore rough clothes, except for his boots and holster. Both of those were Mexican, fine-tooled leather. Even a thin gray layer of trail dust could not obscure the workmanship. The gun, too, an Army Colt, tricked out with ivory grips, was a fine weapon. It was a gun that someone had taken care in preparing and one in which the owner took obvious care in maintaining.

Not a rancher, Clint thought, more than likely a Wells Fargo rider.

Clint was pouring another drink when the old man from the hotel came in, nodding to him.

"That bath, it's ready," the old man said.

The barkeep turned toward Clint and the old man. Clint raised the bottle slightly to indicate he would be taking it with him. The barkeep nodded back and returned to his conversation with the stranger.

"Got a damn fine cathouse in this town," the old man volunteered as they walked the short distance back to the hotel. "Six girls, most of them got most of their teeth. And you come calling on the right day—they don't stink so bad."

"That's good to know," Clint said, smiling.

"Only good to know if you got money in your pocket," the old man said. "Woman that runs the place, mean. Plain mean. No credit, no how."

Clint pushed into the hotel lobby, and the manager scuttled out from behind the desk to show him the way out back to the kitchen and the bath.

Naked as a jay, Clint eased himself into the warm water and settled in, bottle in one hand, soap in the other. It had only been two days since his last warm bath, but that business on the trail, with the horse dying and the walk into town, left him needing some relaxing.

He lay in the bath for a long time, sipping and thinking, the whiskey warming his insides and the bath warming his outsides.

Presently, the manager came in. "Pardon the intrusion. Have you given any thought to them clothes?"

"Clothes," Clint repeated, his voice sounding lazy and heavy with whiskey in his own ears.

"The brushing, sir," the manager said.

Clint thought for a moment, took another sip of the whiskey, and said, "Hell, why not? Brush 'em out. Do it good now."

"Yes, sir," the manager said and gathered up the dusty duds.

Best thing, Clint thought, was to head on down the trail. Maybe make out for Reno or Candelaria. Look for a town that offered more work. Then, with thoughts of larger towns still running through his head, he drifted into a whiskey sleep.

When he awoke, the bathwater was cold and his

THE POSSE FROM ELSINORE

clothes were laid out in front of him, hung proper on a chair and looking somewhat better.

Clint took a long pull from the bottle to take the chill of the cooling water off, then ducked his head under the water once before climbing from the tin tub.

TWO

The room wasn't much more than a narrow scrap of space with a narrow cot in it. Not much bigger than a grave, really. All it had to recommend it was the fact of the cot, clean sheets, and a door. That's the way they built them when they built during boom days, Clint thought. They built as many as they could, halving the size of what would be a small room. They built them small and charged dearly and no one complained.

By the time Clint opened the door to the tomblike room, he didn't give a damn. He'd already finished better than half the bottle, and the bed with its clean sheets was about the best thing he could imagine.

He shut the door behind him, sent the bolt home, then made for the bed. His gear was set out on the bed, like he wanted, and soon he learned why. There wasn't enough room on either side of the bed for the saddle. So he wedged the saddle between the bed and the door and fell into a deep sleep. The last thought in his head before sleep ambushed him was the scent of the dead horse the saddle had left on the sheets.

When he awoke, the thin sliver of a window above his bed was darkened with the night sky. There was no way of telling how long he had slept, only that he felt better than he had in a long time. He moved slowly from the bed, throwing his feet off the edge, then moving in the dark to where he remembered the door. He tripped once, cursing at the saddle that blocked his progress, then threw it back up on the cot, before sliding back the bolt and opening the door.

The lamp in the narrow hall was lit and above it he saw a clock that gave the time as a quarter past ten. Not so very late, he thought, not if you weren't a farmer or a rancher. Not too late for those in town.

He made his way down the stairs into the small lobby of the hotel. The manager behind his desk, polishing at the bell, acknowledged Clint with a curt nod.

"There a place to get a meal?" Clint asked, coming up to the desk, working the last bit of sleep from his legs.

"Could try down at the saloon," the manager answered. "Had a good supper here tonight. I could have the cook make you up a plate. Beefsteak, greens, and biscuits. That is, if you don't mind taking your supper in the kitchen."

"I done worse," Clint answered. "Call the cook, I'm about ready to eat that bell of yours."

The manager made a small, reflexive motion toward the bell, then rang it. "Imagine drinking in the middle of the day would make a man hungry," he said.

Clint eyed the little man. He had seen his type before. They wore clean shirts and oiled their hair. They bathed regular and fussed constantly. More often than not someone with cleaner shirts and more oil in their hair had given them something to be in control of. As far as Clint could see, this peckerwood was in control of about a pound and a half of brass bell.

"Didn't mean nothing personal by it, understand?" the little fat man said. "Nothing a'tall."

"A man's drinking *is* personal," Clint answered. "I'll be sitting a spell over there in that corner. You let me know when my supper's ready."

Clint was halfway across the small lobby when the old man came from the kitchen and exchanged a few whispered words with the manager. Then, as Clint was taking his place in one of the corner chairs, where the loafers had sat earlier in the day, the batwings swung open and a stranger stepped into the hotel.

"What can I do you for, sir?" the manager asked, hoping he'd have more luck in the manners department with this stranger than with Clint.

"Room, a bottle, and a five-dollar whore," the man answered.

Clint watched the stranger carefully. He was average height, dressed in rough clothes and a broad, low-crowned black Stetson. But what caught Clint's eye in particular was the man's side arm. It was a Smith & Wesson single-action .44 with walnut grips. It hung in a battered quick-draw–style holster. Cleaned and oiled recently, the gun gleamed in the dull yellow lamplight of the hotel.

Two of them, Clint thought. Two in one day. Wasn't often you saw two men with guns like that in one day in one town. Both of them, the Colt and the Smith & Wesson, weren't farmers' or ranchers' weapons.

Clint was thinking about the gun when the old man hobbled over to where he sat and tapped his arm. "Beefsteak is cooked for you," he said. "Best eat it while it's hot."

Clint followed the old man through the swinging door to the kitchen as the stranger walked heavily up the stairs to his room.

"This old town, you should have seen her, three, four years back," the old man said. "Ah, she was something then. Really something."

The cook, a fat woman, hunched over the stove, working at some task, while Clint and the old-timer ate. Clint dug into the steak with knife and fork both to haul huge bloody chunks of the thick meat up to his mouth. The old man, near toothless Clint now realized, sopped gravy from a pan with a stale biscuit.

"Good times, huh, old-timer?" Clint asked, around a mouthful of meat.

"Good times, hell, the best times," the old man answered. "Not likely to see the likes again. Not like that. Dig a nugget big as a mule out of the ground. Won't see times like that again."

"Not much here anymore, is there?" Clint asked.

"Got the railroad, a course," the old man said. "That spur head's a blessing. Wells Fargo station. Couple of spreads just north. Not much anymore. Hotel's busier than I seen in a while, though. That's something."

Clint cut another piece of meat. It was tough, old meat. "Me and that other is it?"

"You and *two* others," the old man said, stuffing another piece of soaked doughy biscuit into his maw. "Damn, I ain't seen the likes for a couple months. You boys not being railroad, that is."

"The other, he a tall fella, red hair, beard?" Clint asked, chewing.

"That's him, that's the one."

"They know each other?" Clint asked.

"Not that I could see. Both paid in full, up front, just like you."

"Nothing peculiar in that."

"Not the ways I can see, anyway."

Clint ate in silence for a long time, listening to the old man's stories of the way the town was and never would be again. He was just finishing up his steak when the sheriff came through the doors. The lawman was a big man with a large belly. But Clint guessed he could still handle his own.

"Howdy," the sheriff said, reaching a finger to his hat brim. Then to the old man, "Zeke. You behaving yourself?"

"I'm an old man, Sheriff, I ain't got much of a choice now, have I?"

The sheriff stood there for a long moment, studying Clint. Then without taking his eyes off him, he said,

"Zeke, I believe I heard your bell. You better attend to it."

The old man didn't question the order; rather, he stuffed the last morsel of food into his mouth and headed toward the door.

The sheriff took the old man's chair, reversing it to lean his arms on its ladder back. "Old Zeke filling your ears with how it used to be, was he?"

"We talked a spell," Clint said.

"Old Zeke was here . . . what was it? Three or four years ago when I came in," the sheriff said. "Truth is, Elsinore wasn't ever much more than this."

"This isn't too bad," Clint said.

"No, not too bad," the lawman agreed. "Quiet. That ain't too bad for any town."

"No, sir, it isn't."

"Truth is, a town, any town is like a man, soon as it grows up. Gets as big as it's gonna be, it starts dying. Same as a man. You figuring on staying or passing through?"

"Passing through," Clint answered.

"Ah, that's good then," the sheriff said. "Not much opportunity for a man here. See you got yourself a nice piece of meat. Did some drinking. Had yourself a warm bath. Probably find yourself down at the edge of town tonight. That's the best we got to offer for someone passing through."

Clint finished chewing the last of the steak and pushed the plate forward. "You make that speech to everyone or just me?" he asked.

"Mostly everyone," the lawman answered plainly. "Old Harvey, he saw you set into drinking, got a mite

THE POSSE FROM ELSINORE

worried. He don't want no trouble any more than I do . . . most likely any more than you."

"I don't want any trouble at all, Sheriff," Clint said.

"See, that's nice," the lawman answered. "That's what I like to hear."

Having said what he came to say, the lawman sighed heavily, rose from the chair, turned it back into the table, and started for the door. "You enjoy Elsinore now," he said. "Have yourself a fine time before moving on."

Clint sat waiting until he was certain the sheriff was gone from the hotel. He couldn't say that he blamed the lawman. The town was quiet and he had a right to a quiet town. It was just that Clint didn't care much for being warned, no matter how friendly or in the right the person doing the warning was.

Eventually Clint rose from the table and made his way out of the hotel.

It was a cool, clear night. Walking down the boards toward the saloon, Clint passed the sheriff's office. The lawman was seated outside, tilted back on a stool, smoking a cheroot. He raised his fingers to his hat brim, acknowledging Clint. "Just keep on going, straight down to the end," he said lazily, assuming Clint was heading for the cathouse.

"Thank you, Sheriff," Clint answered and kept walking, feeling the lawman's eyes on his back. He didn't feel like explaining to the man his reasons for not going to the bordello. Clint had never paid for sex, and he didn't aim to start now.

He could see the lights of the cathouse at the edge of town, but he turned into the saloon, hoping to find some female companionship that didn't come with a price tag attached.

THREE

Just as Clint was about to enter the saloon, another man stepped out. He was a tall man, smartly dressed in a dark suit coat and gold embroidered vest, a thin cigar stuck between his lips. Even done up in those slick clothes, the man had a hungry, feral look to him that Clint noticed immediately.

Smiling suddenly and broadly, the man spread both arms, blocking the doorway to the saloon. "Stranger, you don't want to go in there, it's near dead. I can see you're a hale and hearty fella, the place for you is over yonder." With that the man turned Clint toward the cathouse.

"Hold on—"

"Name's DeGraw, Dewit DeGraw. Walk with me, friend."

Clint found himself being led along the boardwalk to the bordello.

"And you are?"

"Clint. Clint Adams."

"Well, Clint Adams, that cathouse yonder happens to be the finest of establishments. How do I know? I own the place."

They stood before a small cottage house, nicely painted, with a white picket fence around it. DeGraw opened the gate and ushered Clint into the yard.

"Seeing as you're obviously new in town, I'd like to buy you a drink."

Clint stopped on the steps. "I appreciate that. But, Mr. DeGraw—"

"Dewit!"

"Dewit, I should tell you before we step inside that I'm not in the habit of paying for sex."

"What!" DeGraw looked around as if afraid someone would hear. "You trying to ruin me with an attitude like that?"

Clint had to smile. "Nope."

"Well, come on in anyway. Maybe you'll change your mind."

"Not likely," Clint said, but he followed DeGraw in, curious in spite of himself.

DeGraw had a small caliber side arm on his hip. Clint didn't recognize the model, but he'd seen pearl handles like that before. He wondered if it was for show or if DeGraw knew how to use it.

Inside the parlor there were three or four girls and two men, ranchers or foremen, Clint guessed. They were spread out on the sofas and chairs, joking with one another.

"Folks, ladies and gentlemen, I want you all to meet Clint Adams," DeGraw said, with some graciousness. "He's new in town. So you all take advantage of his company, 'cause no telling how long we'll have that privilege."

There were a few howdies, and Clint removed his hat and took a seat.

"Mr. Adams, how about that drink? Maybe a cigar?"

Clint asked for both and settled back in the chair. If this was the way they did it in Elsinore, Clint wasn't going to argue. There was an unhurried pleasantness about it. Not exactly a church social, but not the usual rushed commerce of a typical whorehouse.

After chatting for a bit, Clint noticed that the two men didn't appear to know each other. One was a rancher, in town for the Wells Fargo coach the next day and the payment for ten head of steer he'd sold the month before.

But the other one—something bothered Clint about him. He seemed to know neither DeGraw or the rancher, a fella named Crimick. He was wearing a worn set of trail clothes, but he appeared freshly bathed, like Clint. He was maybe fifty, maybe a little younger. His blond hair was streaked with gray, and he stared at Clint cageylike, catching glimpses when he thought Clint's attentions were turned toward a joke DeGraw was telling or toward one of the girls. It was like he was sizing him up, trying to figure something out.

The blond man held his tongue, as well, not speaking unless addressed. Clint knew that a quiet man was not necessarily someone to fear, but there was a quietness that held something, like the mouth of a cave or a rat hole.

After two drinks and a damned fine cigar, Clint noticed one of the girls sitting on the sofa, a pretty thing with reddish hair and a slim waist, looking his way. From conversation, Clint knew that she called herself May, which had led to many old jokes, all of which got a laugh during the introductions.

May got up, walked over to him, and sat on the arm of his chair. "Dewit told us you're not a paying customer."

"I'm afraid not," Clint said.

"Aren't we attractive enough for you?"

"Oh, definitely," Clint said, eyeing her impressive cleavage. "I just don't like to be with a woman unless I'm sure she wants to be with me. For herself. Not for money."

"Well, I'd sure like to be with you." She looked around the parlor. "And since Dewit seems to be off somewhere sampling his own merchandise, what do you say you and I sneak off and get acquainted?"

Clint was tempted, but he hesitated.

"And if you offer me so much as two bits, I'll be highly insulted."

Clint smiled and stood up.

May took Clint's hand and led him down a narrow hall toward a small room.

When she opened the door, there was another surprise. Not only was the room more than twice the size of the one he occupied at the hotel, but it was furnished in fine young lady fashion, complete with a wall of samplers and doilies set out on a comfortable chair.

"Why don't you sit down and let me get them boots, darling?" May asked.

Clint sat down.

She knelt before him then and slowly pulled off first one boot then the other. She smiled, looking up at him with wide eyes as she did this.

Clint stood and unbuckled his holster, and she carefully drew it off him, handling the gun with care as she placed it on the dresser. "I myself never cared much for guns," she said, returning to him. "I admire a man who knows how to use one, though."

She came to him then, moving into his arms as she pressed herself against him.

Clint could feel the hefty bulk of her breasts as she pushed them into his chest. He could feel them through the thin cotton dress of flowered pattern that she wore.

Then she stepped back, just a small step, and began unfastening the buttons on Clint's shirt, letting her small narrow fingers linger along his chest for just a moment before moving on to the next button.

When she had finished unfastening all of the buttons, she stepped forward again and pressed her cheek against his firm chest while drawing the shirt down around his shoulders before finally letting it drop to the floor.

May stepped back again and looked down poutingly at her own clothing. "Would you care to help a lady?" she asked, indicating the neat row of small buttons that ran down the front of her dress.

Clint figured she'd had enough practice with the buttons but played along anyway, enjoying the little drama of undressing.

He reached out and began unbuttoning the dress. He parted the material a bit and leaned forward to kiss the smooth milky tops of her breasts where they protruded above the lacy bodice.

"You are," she said breathlessly, "a gentleman in every way I can imagine."

Just as the sport of unfastening the buttons was beginning to tire, somewhere around where the bodice ended, she shrugged gently and the brightly colored dress whispered to the floor, revealing a pair of long, pale legs and the remainder of the bodice.

"You are a sight," Clint said. "Oh, yes, you are."

She posed briefly, one leg coming up on tiptoe like one of those French etchings he'd seen, then came back into his arms.

Clint held her tight, drawing her into him firmly. He kissed her, letting his tongue slide into her waiting mouth to meet her own. Then he reached down and felt the ready wetness between her legs. With the touch of his hand, she opened her legs wider and pressed herself against his exploring fingers.

"You have me at a disadvantage," she said, her voice gone husky with lust, when they finally broke off the kiss.

Then she knelt before him and went to work on the buttons at the front of his trousers. Smiling up at him, she worked open the buttons slowly, first one, then another, and another. And on each one, he could feel her fingers tremble and fumble slightly through the material to his now throbbing member.

When she had unfastened all of the buttons, Clint lowered his trousers and stepped out of them, his manhood springing rigid, inches from her face.

"Now, what is it we have here?" She giggled, her hand slowly reaching up to stroke the underside of his member with her soft, warm palm.

Clint felt his knees begin to go soft with a kind of aching lust and moved a step back to sit himself down on the bed.

She crawled forward the half step, continuing to stroke his throbbing member. Then quite unexpectedly, she brought one hand down between her legs. When she brought it up again, it was wet and she held his member with it, sliding her palm up and down, slickening the hard shaft.

Clint abandoned himself to her tender ministrations. He stretched full out across the bed, feeling her hands work their way up and down his shaft.

She paused briefly, and Clint, through slitted eyes, watched as she loosened the fasteners of her bodice, releasing the hefty bulk of her breasts. Edging herself upward a little, she grasped both breasts on either side and captured his now slick shaft between them.

She worked his shaft slowly, sliding it between her large breasts, the pink nipples swollen. She used her entire body, rocking herself back and forth.

Then she removed her breasts and took his member into her mouth. Her hands kneading the tight muscles of his thighs, she captured the head of his shaft between her lips and let it rest there for a long moment, her tongue playing around the tip, before taking its entire length into her mouth.

She held the entire bulk of his hardened penis in her throat for a long time, then slowly drew her head back, letting gleaming inch upon inch slide between her full lips.

And then she repeated it, her entire body moving slowly at first, and then faster and faster, until the shaft was sliding smoothly in and out of her mouth.

Just when Clint felt he could stand no more, she stopped. A moment later, she was crawling upon him, straddling his legs, and then guiding the spit-slick member into her.

Using her knees she began rocking again, slowly at first, then faster and faster. Clint responded with his hips, rising to meet her as a low moan escaped her throat.

He reached up then, his hands finding her large breasts, his thumbs seeking to tease the sweet pink nipples. She moaned louder and he felt her clench inside again and again.

Seconds later, Clint himself felt the sweet release as his hips rose high up off the bed. A short scream escaped her mouth and she clenched down on him hard, draining the last from his hard shaft.

Afterwards, she collapsed on top of him and snuggled deep into his arms.

"I declare, stranger, that was the best ride I've had in quite a while," she said, a smile on her face. "They all as good as you where you come from? If they are I can't imagine the girls letting them leave town."

Clint held her tight, drawing her into his side, feeling her heart beat steady beside him. Her mouth was drawn up into a satisfied smile as she drifted off to sleep.

FOUR

Clint awoke early with a bright morning sun streaming in through the whorehouse curtains. Opening his eyes, warily at first, he saw May sleeping beside him. She had that same smile on her face, and one of her breasts was exposed above the top of the blanket.

Without disturbing the girl, Clint dressed and closed the door gingerly behind him. It had been one hell of a night. The best in recent memory. And a damn sight better than spending the night in that coffin the hotel called a room.

Making his way back out through the parlor, he heard the noise of conversation coming from the kitchen. Slowly, he pushed the door open, thinking to pay his respects and take his leave of whoever was up and about in the early hours of the morning.

It was, he saw once the door was open, the entire whorehouse. DeGraw sat at the head of the kitchen table, surrounded by the two whores he remembered from the night before and a few others he assumed were working when he came calling.

If Clint hadn't known better, he would have thought that DeGraw was a young widowed rancher with a family of young girls. Gone was DeGraw's fancy gold braided vest, replaced by a somber black suit and white shirt. He looked, for all the world, like the most prosperous man in town, which, in fact, he might have been.

"Morning," DeGraw called, then popped a hunk of ham steak into his mouth from the end of his fork. "Figured I'd let you and May bunk down together last night. Consider it a free sample."

"Appreciated," Clint answered.

"I declare, May always has all the luck," one of the whores, a little blond, said.

"Judging from the noise she was making, I'd say," another one, a brown-haired girl with a heart-shaped face, replied. "I been listening to her through the wall going on two years now, and I ain't heard anything like that noise yet."

"Clint, sit yourself down and have some breakfast," DeGraw said. "Damned better than anything you'll likely get at the saloon or that sorry excuse for a rattrap they call a hotel."

"That's true, Mr. Adams, we got the best whiskey, food, cigars, and other entertainments in town," the blond girl said with a sly smile.

THE POSSE FROM ELSINORE 31

Clint tipped his hat, grateful for the invitation, and took a seat opposite DeGraw.

A moment later, a plate of food was put in front of him and he commenced eating. He had to admit, the food did look better than what he had had the day before. And it tasted a damn sight better, too.

"How do you find the hospitality in Elsinore, Mr. Adams?" the brown-haired girl asked.

"Just fine, better all the time," Clint answered, cutting into the ham steak. "Better and better. And this food is the best thing I've eaten in a long time."

"Not surprising, considering what the hotel serves its paying customers," the blond girl said.

A couple of the girls giggled, then held back, staring at their plates.

"I thought," Clint said, taking a bite of the sweet ham, "this place was owned by a woman."

"Fella in town told you that?" DeGraw asked. "I'd bet on it. My last dollar."

"Matter of fact . . ."

"Old gent, was he?" DeGraw continued. "Stooped over, like, with a beard?"

"That's right," Clint said.

"Truth is, this place was owned by Miss Polly," DeGraw answered. "That was six, seven years ago. I bought her out. Threw out that pack of thieving girls she had working for her, stealing her blind, and hired these lovelies. All the way from Seattle. She's living in San Francisco now. Respectable. Runs a boardinghouse, show people I heard."

"Six years, you say?" Clint asked, chewing the ham.

"Hell, old Zeke can't get it through his head Polly don't own the place no more," DeGraw continued. "Comes around every once in a while. Manages to get fifty cent or a dollar together. Can't get it through his head prices go up. He's harmless enough. People round here take care of him. Food, bed, that kind of thing."

"I heard all the noise, chatting and laughing," May said suddenly from the doorway.

She was dressed in a red robe, her hair pinned up.

"Sleep half the day away there, May," DeGraw said. "This young buck tire you out? I'll say, truthful now. One of my favorite things is breakfast in a whorehouse in the middle of the afternoon."

"Let's just say there was less sleep than usual," she answered, smiling as she went to fetch herself a cup of coffee from the stove, lingering there and surveying the scene around the breakfast table.

A few of the girls giggled some more.

"What exactly is it that brings you to Elsinore?" DeGraw asked Clint.

"A dead horse," Clint answered, sipping his coffee.

"Neat trick, that," DeGraw said, smiling. "There a story behind it?"

Clint told the story then of the horse dying and him having to walk the few remaining miles, then added that the walk had been worth the trouble.

"So, you plan on heading along then?" one of the girls asked, the blonde.

"I reckon I do," Clint said. "Figure to buy a new horse to get me back home. Never should have left my own horse, Duke, behind. I'll probably head out at noon. Get a few miles before dark.''

"I know a fella, he has a horse he'd be willing to part with," DeGraw said. "He's in town. Be glad to make the introductions for you."

"Appreciated," Clint answered.

"I'm coming with you then," May said. "I need to look at something down at the general merchandise."

"What would that be?" the blond girl asked.

"It isn't none of your business, now is it?"

"It wouldn't be our friend Mr. Adams here, now, would it?" the girl with the brown hair teased.

"Girls, now please," DeGraw put in. "May's coming with Mr. Adams and myself, that's what's to it. And I don't want to hear any arguments."

The two other girls shut up.

They all ate a slow, unhurried breakfast, lingering over second and third cups of coffee. Then, one by one, the girls started to drift off, back to their rooms and out into the house to do chores.

Clint saw that each girl had her own chores and they went to them uncomplaining.

Finally, there was just May, Clint, and DeGraw sitting at the table.

A little time later, Clint, May, and DeGraw exited the house and crossed the narrow strip of dirt to the boards.

"It's like this, Clint," DeGraw said. "The so-called respectable women in town, now, they don't object to a cathouse. They're practical women. The thing they do object to is the girls running around unescorted. And I oblige them. I've found in my business what most people object to isn't what they'd label sin. It's the appearance of sin that gets them in those self-righteous moods."

"We've reached what you'd call an understanding," May said. "Long as we do our business in the house and don't frighten the horses, they let us stay."

"Let us stay, hell," DeGraw put in. "I judged the pie baking contest three years running."

Clint heard the words but didn't focus on them. A little ahead and to the right, he saw three men congregated on the other side of the street. They were the two strangers, with the fancy side arms, and the blond man from last night.

"Clint, I don't believe you've heard a word we've said," May joked, pulling Clint's arm.

"You know them?" Clint said, turning to DeGraw.

DeGraw shook his head no. "That one there, on the left, he was in last night," he said. "Didn't spend more than an hour and five dollars. The others, can't say I ever saw them."

Clint let his eyes drift across from where the men were standing. Directly in front of them was the Wells Fargo office. "Stage due today, isn't it?"

DeGraw said, "Any minute."

They kept strolling up the boards, May talking to Clint, but him not hearing her. Clint's attention was focused on the three men.

"What's coming in on that stage?" Clint asked. "You know anything about that?"

DeGraw paused, thinking. "Mail, geegaws for the

general merchandise. Some mail-ordered suits, I expect," he answered. "Same as usual. Couple years ago there'd be money, gold and such going in and out. Not anymore. All the gold that comes in on that stage leaves on it."

"What do you mean?" Clint asked. "That there's gold on the stage?"

"Hell yeah, ten thousand maybe, heading up north. It just rides on through."

"I swear, sometimes it seems the whole world just passes through," May said. "People would like this town, if they took the time to appreciate it properly, Clint. Isn't that right, Dewit?"

"That's the truth, May," DeGraw answered slowly and lazily.

"That's the main thing, though, they got to take the time. All the good things just pass through. And that ain't right," May said, giving Clint a long look which he either ignored or didn't see.

"Every time or just once in a while?" Clint asked, watching as one of the men moved away from the trio and crossed the street to take up a position a little ways down the boards from the Wells Fargo office.

"Like I told you, they always carry gold but not for Elsinore," DeGraw said. "None to speak of, anyways. Why? This town hasn't seen any gold in a long time. Creek about two miles up in the hills, that had some gold, for a while. No more. If it wasn't for where we were, heading north and south and the rail spur, we'd be nothing but dust and broken-down buildings."

"And we ain't much more than that now," May offered.

But Clint wasn't listening to the lazy talk. Three horses were hitched on the street. Two on the opposite side, one near the Wells Fargo office. All three had saddlebags, bedrolls. There were other horses on the street, but these three stood out from the lot because they weren't the typical broken-down ranch animals.

"Funny thing to see three horses hitched with saddlebags and bedrolls in the middle of the day, isn't it?" Clint asked. "You find anything strange about that?"

DeGraw shrugged. "I can't say that it is," he said. "Probably belong to them three over there. Probably getting ready to move on. Folks don't stay long."

"Ain't that the truth," May said, speaking up as she took Clint's arm. "Ride in and ride out. Always on the way someplace else."

It was just then that Clint heard the low rumble of the stage. It was the only sound on the otherwise quiet street.

"You wearing your gun?" Clint asked DeGraw.

"What are you talking about?" May put in.

"You wearing a gun?" Clint asked again, ignoring May.

"Not likely," DeGraw said. "Middle of the day. I put it on when the sun goes down and the drinking starts."

"Go get one," Clint said.

FIVE

"What do you mean, 'go get one'?" DeGraw asked, stopping.

"They're going to rob the stage," Clint said.

"What? Friend, I don't know what May did to you last night, but—"

"Go get a gun!" Clint spat out. "And the sheriff."

"Clint, darling," May said.

And then the stage rounded onto the street from the trail. Clint watched as one of the three took up a position near the Wells Fargo office while another lingered on the opposite side of the street, near the horses. The third one began a slow, cautious walk toward the middle of the street, his eyes staying on the stage.

DeGraw had not moved. He stood where he was,

watching the driver pull the horses up in front of the Wells Fargo office.

A second later, the manager of the office came out, wearing a green visor and a clean white shirt.

"Go get the sheriff," Clint said.

"Friend, you're crazy," DeGraw said, still not moving.

Later, much later, Clint would wonder if the whole thing wouldn't have turned out differently if DeGraw had listened to him.

There were a couple of loafers out on the boards, but not many. The old man from the hotel pushed out through the doors, so did the manager.

The shotgun rider jumped down from the stage, leaving the ten-gauge in the boot. The moment he hit the ground, all hell broke loose.

The first shot came from Clint's side of the street. It caught the shotgun rider dead center in his chest, spinning him slightly and sending his body back toward the stage's wheels.

The second shot came from the middle of the street, from the gunman who was cautiously crossing. The big slug caught the driver on the jaw, exploding it in a spray of blood and bone. The driver slumped forward, reaching for the shotgun. His hands were almost to the stock when the gunman in front of the Wells Fargo office fired into his skull.

It wasn't until the third shot that the horses panicked. The lead horse whinnied in terror and stepped forward, but the gunman in the street grabbed the reins quickly.

The Wells Fargo agent, stunned, started to say

something as he stepped forward and was rewarded with a bullet in the side of the head for his effort.

The third gunman was bringing the horses around now; he was up on a claybank and leading the other two forward, ready for the fast ride out of town.

Clint drew and fired at the gunman who shot the Wells Fargo clerk, the bullet catching him on the arm. The blond man startled and fired back, and Clint dove into the street, putting the stage between him and the gun. He came up fast, gun pointed at the street, as another shot from the outlaw holding the horses kicked up a small plume of dust in front of Clint.

Rolling, Clint fired twice at the outlaw holding the horses, then rolled under the stage. Above him, he heard a gunman curse as he dropped the heavy strongbox to the boards. Another shot and the lock was sprung open.

Three feet from where Clint lay under the stage, the dead clerk's eyes stared unseeing from where he lay on the boards.

Then there was running on the boards and a voice that Clint recognized as the sheriff's called out. Two more shots, and then a blast from a rifle.

Clint crawled to the back of the stage, then out from under and crouched there, waiting for a gunman to appear. He could see clear down the street, but no gunman. Peeking out from one side, he saw the outlaw with the horses leading them quickly away.

Leaping up, Clint climbed atop the stage from the rear. A shot rang out and a section of wood splintered a few inches from his eyes.

"DeGraw!" he shouted, crawling over the leather satchels secured to the top of the stage.

"Here!" came the reply from a doorway.

Coming over the top of the stage, Clint spied DeGraw and May huddled in a doorway. A few doorways down the street, a gunman held a similar position. The outlaw with the horses had vanished, disappeared around the corner of the building. Clint could not see the third but knew him to be close by.

Clint made his way toward the seat and reached for the ten-gauge. Another shot pounded into the dead driver. The big ten-gauge was a few inches out of Clint's grasp.

Firing two shots toward the gunman in the doorway, he leapt forward, grabbed the shotgun from its boot, and tossed it to DeGraw.

Another shot sounded from the doorway, striking the stage low and splintering wood. The horses, sensing the passage of the bullet, reared and stamped. Then the lead horse bolted in a wide-eyed panic.

Clint grabbed the reins and pulled, unmindful of everything, even the gunman in the doorway. The animals' fear came up through the thick leather as the stage began gathering speed.

Clint turned in time to see DeGraw raising the shotgun, May huddled behind him against a shopkeeper's locked door. The two barrels of the shotgun came up and for a split second Clint was staring down both; then DeGraw fired.

To Clint it looked like DeGraw had fired directly at him, and it took a second to realize he was still alive. A moment later he was nearly tossed over the front of the stage as the dead third gunman tumbled forward from the top of the stage over Clint's back and into his lap. Half his head was blown away by the powerful scattergun. A single eye hung forlornly halfway down his stubbled cheek.

For an instant the dead man tangled in the reins, very nearly tearing them from Clint's hands. Then Clint kicked him forward, over the front. He fell between the traces, and a second later there was a solid bump as the wheels ran over his body. He *was* close all right, spitting distance.

Clint put his back and arms into the task now, pulling up powerfully on the reins, fighting the team's blind fear. Yet the wagon continued to gather speed.

Then there was another shotgun blast. Clint turned and saw, incredibly, the outlaw who a few moments ago had positioned himself in the doorway, running. He was running alongside the coach on the boards, nearly even.

Clint reached for his gun, but the corpse had knocked it from the seat beside him to the floorboards. To let loose of the reins was suicide. The horses, free from the pull of the leather, would tip the stage and drag it along the street.

For a brief instant, they were even, Clint and the outlaw, and Clint could see the wild panic in the man's eyes, the desperate fear that mirrored the fear of the horses.

Then the man turned, his boots slipping as he rounded the corner, and Clint caught a glimpse of the gunman with the horses as the coach sped past the alleyway.

* * *

It took a quarter of a mile to bring the team under control. Clint, sitting up in the motionless coach, reins still in his hands, began breathing again.

Maybe a half a minute elapsed before he heard the shouts of men running toward him. When they finally reached the coach, Clint gladly surrendered the reins and picked his side arm up from the floorboards.

As they walked slowly back to the Wells Fargo office, one of the men offered to buy him a drink, another slapped him on the back.

"We got one of 'em by God," one of the men said. "We got one of 'em."

Clint looked at the man, a plump little shopkeeper with a long apron. More than likely the man had cowered in his store during the robbery. Probably hiding behind a barrel of brooms or a bolt of gingham.

The dead men lay on the boards and in the street where they had fallen. The sheriff went from one to the other, inspecting grimly, ignoring the advice of the small crowd that had gathered.

DeGraw and May were sitting on a bench outside the Wells Fargo office. The shotgun was still on DeGraw's lap. May hung on his arm fiercely.

Oddly, the box of gold coins lay open on the boards, tipped on its side. The coins spilled out across the wood, shining in the afternoon sun. Easily ten thousand or more. Clint could tell that without even looking twice. Nobody seemed to pay it any mind. Ten thousand in gold lying on the ground like trash, and every loafer and storekeeper in town gawking wide-eyed at dead men.

THE POSSE FROM ELSINORE 43

"I need a wagon here!" the sheriff bellowed.

None of the men surrounding him moved.

"I said I need a wagon here!" the lawman repeated.

Still nobody moved, beyond shuffling their boots in the dust.

"God, I'm so glad you're alive," May said, leaving DeGraw's arm and hugging Clint.

"I guess I owe you an apology," DeGraw said. "How'd you know?"

"Firearms," Clint said. "Three strangers carrying tricked-out side arms like that. Not likely in a place like this, unless they were together and looking to break the law."

"I need a wagon here!" the sheriff bellowed again.

"There's gonna be hell to pay," DeGraw said. "Wells Fargo office in San Francisco doesn't take kindly to men killing its employees."

Clint followed DeGraw's stare to the dead Wells Fargo clerk. He lay a few feet away, the front of his white shirt stained bright with blood, the wire glasses still on his face.

"The others, they got away?"

"Had the horses around there." Clint pointed. "They hit that trail. They could head north or south."

"They'll go north," DeGraw said. "Won't go back to San Francisco."

"Damn it, get me a damned wagon!" came the sheriff's call now. "Haul this out of the street!"

Clint looked over. Men had retreated back to the boards; the sheriff stood alone in the center of the street with the dead bodies.

"Let 'em rot then, for all I give a damn!" the sheriff said and stormed off the street.

The sheriff walked to where the Wells Fargo clerk lay. He looked down on him with a vague sadness. "He wasn't a bad sort," the lawman said. "Quiet. Kept to himself mostly."

Then the lawman knelt down, gently removed the spectacles from his face, placed them in the clerk's vest pocket, and with his thumbs closed the man's eyes. "Damn, if this ain't been a bad day in Elsinore," the sheriff said.

"I ain't seen worse," DeGraw said.

Then the sheriff went to his knees again and began gathering up the gold and putting it in the strongbox. He did this somberly, a man who had just seen his street littered with bodies and was handling money he knew he couldn't keep.

"You men, give me a hand with this," the lawman said when he had put all the gold in the box and closed the lid.

Clint and DeGraw rose and carried the box to the sheriff's office. May, holding the ten-gauge DeGraw had handed to her, followed behind.

They put the money box down in the cool of the sheriff's office and took seats in front of the sheriff's desk. May handed the shotgun over to the lawman and sat down in a chair by the window.

The fat lawman put his rifle in the rack and sat behind the desk.

"Damn it, we're just going to have to do something about this," he said. "Something's gotta be done."

"You looking for a posse, Sheriff?" DeGraw asked.

"I may be, I just may be," the lawman answered, then closed his eyes tight.

"Count me deputized then," DeGraw said.

The sheriff opened his eyes, stared at Clint. "You, too?"

"Me, too," Clint said.

"Pardon my asking, but this ain't your town," the sheriff replied. "Wasn't none of your gold, either, was it? I don't see where it's personal to you."

"Not my town and not my gold," Clint replied. "But it was my skin they were shooting at. I count that pretty personal."

The sheriff nodded and closed his eyes again. When he opened them he said, "By the power vested in me as sheriff of Elsinore, I deputize both of you. Allowing for all the rights and privileges which go along with it, including shooting those two sons of bitches that killed the Wells Fargo clerk and tried to rob the stage."

Clint nodded. It all sounded just fine to him.

SIX

The sheriff had just finished speaking when one of DeGraw's girls, the brown-haired girl with the heart-shaped face, came running into the office. "Sheriff Smith, they shot her!" she screamed. "They shot Lucy. She was out in the back and they just shot her."

DeGraw jumped to his feet and was running down the boards, May right behind him, before either Clint or the sheriff were out the door.

When Clint reached the whorehouse, just before the sheriff, he saw the dead girl. She was on the ground in the flower bed beside the house. DeGraw had turned her over and was holding her head in his hands. There was a neat bullet hole at the center of her forehead, just below her blond hairline.

May was standing behind DeGraw sobbing softly. Other girls formed a loose circle around them.

"She was tending to the flowers, and these men, they rode by and shot her," the brown-haired girl said. "I saw the whole thing from the window. She kinda looked up at them and this fella just shot her."

There was a small spade in the girl's hand. Running from a shoot-out with the law, the outlaws, Clint could imagine, had mistaken it for a gun.

DeGraw closed her eyes and stood up. "They're gonna die, both of them," he said. "That girl, she never did a lick of harm to nobody. Nobody."

Clint judged it to be a half hour since the shooting on the street by the time they found him a horse and wired Wells Fargo as to what had happened.

In that time, two more men came forward to join the posse. One was a clerk in the general merchandise, no more than a boy, really, by the name of Witt. He showed up with a sorry-looking mare and an ancient Army Colt. From the looks of him, he was barely old enough to stroke a razor across his cheek. Clint suspected he was joining the search more from boredom of sweeping out the shop than any sense of civic pride.

The second new member was the son of the town's banker, named Kendal. He was a big one, older than the boy, but not much. There was a meanness about him that you could see if you looked close. He showed up on a fine gelding, sporting a pair of matching pistols from Spain engraved with fine scrollwork up and down the handles.

The thing that surprised Clint the most, though, was Sheriff Smith. When he saddled his horse, he slid a

Sharps English model rifle into a double boot alongside his saddle. The second section of the boot held a mean-looking ten-gauge with polished stock.

"That's a fine-looking rifle, Sheriff," Clint said as they rode out of town, five abreast. DeGraw had fixed Clint up with a roan gelding, but he sorely missed Duke.

"Had this made for me in Mexico a few years back," the lawman answered. "Real handy when you need it."

To hit a man at five hundred yards was nothing for the Sharps and Clint knew it. To even own it meant you weren't planning on getting close to whatever you wanted to kill.

DeGraw, Witt, and Kendal were silent as they reached the trail. The boy was quiet most likely because he didn't have anything to say. DeGraw, he was taking it personal. And Clint just couldn't figure Kendal at all.

Clint noticed, too, that the sheriff didn't ride like a fat man. He sat light in the saddle, ramrod straight. Not what anyone would expect from a lawman accustomed to loafing in front of his office all day.

The tracks, as DeGraw had said, led north once they made the trail at dusk. Two horses, moving quickly.

"They're gonna put as much space between Elsinore and them as quick as they can," the sheriff said, stopping to appraise the tracks. "I give them five miles of hard riding. After that, I don't know."

"Turn up into the hills maybe," DeGraw said. "On one of them Indian trails."

"They could maybe double back on it," Sheriff Smith answered.

Clint thought about it. No, he didn't think they'd double back, start riding south. "I say they're in a hurry to get away from us," he put in. "That's the first ten, maybe twenty miles. After that, they're gonna be in a hurry to find another stage or bank, or what have you."

"You talk like a man who knows this kind," Smith said, giving Clint a hard look, trying to puzzle him out.

"I run into them now and again," Clint said. "If they had gotten the gold, I'd say maybe we could consider them doubling back, heading for San Francisco. Looking for someplace to spend it on liquor and women. Since they didn't get any gold, they'll be looking for someplace to rob. Someplace like Elsinore."

"Well, they picked the wrong damned town," the banker's son, Kendal, said. "The wrong damned town."

The sheriff ignored the boy, thinking. "We'll follow the stage line north. Wells Fargo means a trail of money. We'll follow the money."

The sheriff was right. Five miles outside of town the tracks turned to a pair of walking horses. By dusk they were so hard to read, confused as they were with old tracks on the much-used trail, that the men decided to make camp.

The sheriff, who seemed to know the country well, led them off the trail up a little ways into the hills, where he found a clearing near a small spring.

"I say we should have kept going," the young clerk Witt said. "Follow them and bring them to ground like hunting an animal."

"Slow up, boy," the sheriff answered. "They ain't animals, they're men. That means they're smarter, meaner, and more cunning. You hunt a man like an animal, you're the one whose gonna end up hunted."

Clint, who was building a fire in the clearing, listened. The lawman knew what he was talking about. Maybe he knew too well. Looking up, he reappraised the fat sheriff and saw a shrewdness he hadn't noticed before. "You sound like a man who knows what he's talking about," Clint said.

"I been on a few posses," the sheriff said. "Done my fair share of this kind of work."

"Hell, fair share, ain't you gonna tell him?" the boy said, his arms loaded with deadfall wood as he came back into the clearing.

"Tell me what?" Clint asked.

"Nothing," the lawman said, shooting the boy a sharp look.

Kendal, who was sitting under a tree tending to his fancy pistols, gave a snort that put a crooked smile on his face.

DeGraw went about his job of hobbling the horses.

Suddenly Clint began to wonder what kind of trouble he'd gotten himself into. He didn't much care for being shot at, but he cared less for riding along with men he didn't know and wasn't sure he could trust.

It wasn't until later, after a dinner of biscuits and

salted beef, that the five men sat around the fire, talking of the robbery itself.

"They knew that money was on the stage," Witt said. "That's gotta tell you something."

"Tells you they were like everyone else between San Francisco and Reno," the sheriff remarked. "That stage has been robbed so many times it's a wonder they just don't put the thieves on the payroll."

"That was pretty slick of them," Witt added. "Trying to take it in Elsinore."

"Cowardly is all," the sheriff answered. "That man riding shotgun got the weapon 'cross his lap soon as he climbs on the coach. They picked the only time he put it down to make their move. That's a coward's move, son."

"Probably thought Elsinore would be easy pickin's," Kendal said, spinning the cylinder of his pistol. "They'll regret it. They'll die regretting it."

Clint watched as Kendal continued to play with the fancy firearm. It was as if he could barely control himself from shooting it, shooting something. Anything. Though Clint didn't know the boy's father, it was just like a banker to buy his son a fine set of matching guns, thinking he was buying the lad skill to use them or the character to appreciate what using them meant.

The boy continued to spin the cylinder, hearing it click around at each chamber. Clint thought that stroking them and playing with them like the boy did cheapened the work that went into creating such fine weapons. In his hands they were reduced to something like the cheap, two-dollar pistols drunk saddle tramps waved on payday.

Presently, Witt, the sheriff, and Kendal fell asleep. Clint fed the fire, building it to take off the night chill before he himself turned in. DeGraw sat at the fire's edge lost in thought.

Clint wanted to ask him something but couldn't think of the exact words. Finally he just came out and asked it. "Smith doesn't seem like any small-town sheriff I ever met," he said.

DeGraw looked up across the flames and laughed quietly. "I bet he ain't," DeGraw said. "Not likely you'll meet his kind again anytime soon."

"You want to tell me what he is?" Clint asked, tossing a small branch into the flame.

"Ain't what he is," DeGraw said. "He's the sheriff of Elsinore. Duly elected. Thirty-five votes to thirty-three. Same count running five years in a row. Don't matter who he got running against him. Some people like him, some don't. Those that don't, they're the ones that don't like his past."

"What was he, then?" Clint asked.

DeGraw smiled. "Hell, he knows you're gonna find out sooner or later," he said. "Better me telling you than Witt. He was just about the best damn regulator anybody ever saw."

"That explains that Sharps," Clint said.

"Explains a lot of things," DeGraw answered. "Stock associations, they paid him a hundred, a hundred fifty dollars a week—a week, mind you—to take care of their problems."

"That was a long time ago?" Clint asked.

"Not too long ago," DeGraw said. "More recent than you'd think. A couple of fellas, fancy gents, they rode in last year looking for him. Told one of the girls they'd pay a hundred a week for his services."

"What did he say?"

"They rode out the next day, back just the way they came," DeGraw said. "He didn't ride with them. I took that as an answer."

"That's a lot of money to turn down," Clint said, "a lot of money to pass up to sit out in front of an office in Elsinore."

"The gents, they started talking, too," DeGraw added. "It don't surprise you I hear the stories the girls hear. They told why he came to Elsinore, why he must have turned down the money."

Clint poked the fire with a stick, sending a small plume of sparks rising. "You want to pass that along?" Clint asked. "Just so I know who I'm riding with."

DeGraw thought this last bit over. "Man's got a right to know that," he said at last. Then he told the story.

DeGraw told it the way he had heard it from the girl. The way it started was that Smith was working for a stock association in Wyoming. He was earning a hundred dollars a week just by staying in town and letting it be known he was in town. Then winter hit.

It was a bad winter. A real mean one. Come February, a ranch hand found what was left of a steer butchered up in the hills. Then another one turned up, butchered the same way.

Smith put down his fancy cigars, brandy, and cards to ride out. The second day out, he spotted the rustler. Hell, it was cold and he had the rustler dead to rights. A hundred and fifty yards off, dead steer bleeding in the snow and the son of a bitch working at the carcass with an ax.

Smith fired a shot, aiming high into the branches. He was looking to scare him off, knock some snow on him. But the rustler kept working.

Smith fired a second shot and saw the rustler head to his horse and a gun. When he fired the third shot, he was done warning. The gun took more of the head off than it left on. It wasn't until he got to the body and opened the coat that he saw it was a woman. Husband died a week before from influenza. Two children at the cabin up in the woods. She was trying to feed herself and those kids.

Smith left the kids with a minister and rode out. Quit the work. He didn't stop riding until he hit Elsinore.

"It don't snow much in Elsinore," DeGraw said. "And there ain't much ranching. No snow, no ranching, no rustlers. That's what he was looking for and what he found."

SEVEN

They broke camp at dawn and were in the saddle without so much as a biscuit or cup of coffee beforehand. The sky was just turning a pale blue and the birds were chattering when the five men rode back onto the trail.

Clint and the sheriff rode a little ahead, their eyes set on the ground to the left and right in front of them. The horses moved at a slow but steady gait.

It was now impossible to track the outlaws. The trail's hard-packed earth was a maze of hooves and wagon wheels that gave no clues as to what tracks might be fresh from the day before.

"Heard you talking last night," the sheriff said without lifting his eyes from the ground.

"I supposed you might have," Clint answered.

"I reckon a man's got a right to know who he's

riding with," the lawman said. "I can't fault either you or DeGraw."

Clint nodded but kept his eyes on the ground, looking.

"I can put the story straight," the lawman said. "It weren't the mother I shot. It was the sister. Mother and father both dead. Influenza. Buried in the snow. Couldn't even get them in the ground. Children were close to starving when we found them in the cabin."

Clint kept his head down. The sheriff paused in the story, not waiting for an answer but to gather his strength to continue.

"The girl was sixteen, maybe seventeen," the sheriff said. "Put on a buffalo robe to butcher that steer. The robe made her look bigger than she was. When she made the move toward the horse, probably she was running away. I know she wasn't going for the Winchester I saw in the boot. There wasn't any shells left in it when I checked."

The sheriff spoke in a low, soft voice. There was an odd quality to it, as if he were telling a story that had happened to someone else. Behind, Clint heard Witt, DeGraw, and Kendal talking among themselves.

"Lord, that girl made a mess of the steer," the sheriff said. "Put it down with a Winchester, emptied the gun into it, then tried butchering it with an ax, not knowing where to start. Just knowing it was meat. Knowing her parents were buried behind the cabin in the snow."

Behind him, Clint could hear laughing. Young Witt laughing at a joke. It was the nervous laughter of a young man.

"And there I was, living like a fat hog, drinking brandy and smoking cigars," the sheriff said. "Playing cards every night with the ranchers, my bosses. When I got to the body, there wasn't nothing left of the girl's face. But, by God, I remember the faces of those children when we took them from the cabin. I won't forget those, ever. You listening to me?"

"I'm listening, Sheriff," Clint said, eyes still fixed on the ground.

"Know what they told me, those men, my bosses?" the sheriff said. "They asked me why I was quitting after doing a good job. When I didn't say, they threatened me. Said I'd never work again as a regulator. Just to make sure of that, I beat one to within an inch of his life. He spent eight months in bed with his bones healing."

Clint pulled up on his reins, bringing the horse to a stop.

"I see it," the sheriff said, coming up alongside of Clint.

There, at the side of the trail, were two sets of tracks, leading up off the trail. Clint had not seen the tracks immediately. It was the trampled brush that drew his attention.

Clint and the sheriff waited for the others to reach them, then led their horses up a small incline. The trail of trampled brush was easy to follow.

"We got 'em now," Kendal said, drawing out one of the pistols. "By God, we got 'em now."

Half a mile up the hill, they came to the camp. The fire's coals were still warm. The camp was deserted.

"How long you figure?" the sheriff asked Clint, who was kneeling by the fire.

"Couple of hours maybe," Clint said. "They broke camp just before dawn."

The sheriff got down from his horse and walked a circle around the camp. Broken brush indicated where they had tied their horses for the night. There was nothing to show they'd left any way other than where they came in.

"Missed 'em sumbitches," Kendal said, holstering his pistol. "Missed the sumbitches."

Clint got back up on the horse and followed the sheriff back out onto the trail.

"What do you think?" DeGraw asked, riding up alongside the sheriff and Clint once they reached the trail.

"Like I said, a couple hours," Clint answered. "They're putting some miles between us and them."

"They're on the run," the sheriff said. "I didn't see no food crumbs there, did you? Not near water, either."

"They're gonna have to stop, isn't that right, Sheriff?" Witt said, coming up. "Isn't that right? No food, no water. Probably just made camp there to rest their horses."

"That's what I was thinking, son," the sheriff answered.

"What's the next town?" Clint asked.

"That would be Bloody Spur," the sheriff answered. "Not much to it. Elsinore is a regular city compared to it."

"About ten miles," DeGraw said.

THE POSSE FROM ELSINORE 61

"Do they have a Wells Fargo office?" Clint asked.

"I was thinking the same thing," the sheriff said. "Wire them and let 'em know what we're up to here."

They reached Bloody Spur by noon. The sheriff was right, the small mining town made Elsinore look like San Francisco. The town had two actual wood structures to its credit, the hotel with a saloon and the jail. Beyond those two buildings, the town was a series of canvas shanties and hovels constructed with whatever was at hand.

"Used to be a paradise, this town," the sheriff said as they rode in.

"You're lying," Clint said.

"I'm lying, it never was much," the sheriff admitted with a wry smile. "Figure a couple more years and it won't be anything at all."

A small child, barefoot and dirty, ran out of a shack to watch the five men ride into town. He stood mute at the side of the road, eyes wide at the riders.

"There was a creek up there," DeGraw said. "Miner took a couple ounces of silver out a few years back. This is what happened."

They found the sheriff's office, which also happened to be the Wells Fargo office, and hitched their horses to a busted post outside.

Inside, the sheriff was drunk. He was slumped over a desk that was constructed by placing a board over two barrels. A third barrel served as a chair.

"Damn it, Clyde, wake up," Sheriff Smith called. "You drinking this early in the day?"

"I'm drinkin' if you're buying, stranger," the man answered without raising his head.

"It's me, Smith, you damn drunk, wake up."

"Am awake, just drunk is all," the man said. "You got official business or this a social call?"

Smith walked over to the man, grabbed him by the hair, and raised his head. He was a skinny sort, dressed in shabby clothing. And then Clint got a look at his face. It was the face of a man who wasn't too particular about his whiskey, just so there was a lot of it. His red-rimmed eyes floated up under the heavy lids, exposing the gray-yellow whites.

"Kendal, why'n't you take Witt, ask around, see if anybody saw anything of our boys," the sheriff said. "Me and Adams here will try to clean this mess up."

DeGraw had not followed them inside.

"Yes, sir," Witt said, happy to do anything.

"And while you're at it, see if you can find the Wells Fargo man," the sheriff added. "We're gonna be needing to send a telegraph."

Clint built a small fire in the potbellied stove, and they started in on making Bloody Spur's lawman coffee, trying to sober him up.

Before the fire really got going, another man entered. Like the sheriff, he was skinny also. He wore a set of clothes that may have been fine at one time but had seen better days and those days were maybe years ago.

"Gentlemen," he said. "Quintin Endicott, at your disposal. I was told that my services are required."

"Are you the Wells Fargo man?" Clint asked,

THE POSSE FROM ELSINORE 63

moving away from the drunk lawman and letting the Elsinore sheriff handle him.

"That I am, sir, also the telegraph operator."

Clint realized that Endicott was drunk, as well, but not so far into it as the sheriff. There was a strange sort of shabby dignity to the man. "I need to send a telegraph," Clint said. "San Francisco Wells Fargo office."

"I see," Endicott answered. "Won't you step this way, to the office."

Clint followed him back to a small room, where there was a telegraph on a desk alongside an open bottle of whiskey. Several more whiskey bottles littered the floor.

Endicott took a seat and picked up a small nub of pencil, preparing to write. "And the message would be?" he said, letting the last word hang there.

"Tell them the stage at Elsinore was held up," Clint said. "Tell them their man in Elsinore is dead and that the sheriff and four men are pursuing the killers."

"Quite a long message," the man said. "Quite dramatic, as well."

"Just send it," Clint said, and walked back out into the sheriff's office.

Smith had somehow gotten the man almost sobered up, at least standing up, by the time Clint came back out from the telegraph.

Bloody Spur's sheriff stood in the middle of the room, rubbing his eyes, holster empty, saying, "What's that you're tellin' me? What's that again?"

"Two men, they shot the Wells Fargo clerk, the

driver, the shotgun, and a whore," Sheriff Smith said. "We're tracking them now."

"How many is that all together?" the other sheriff asked. "Four dead is it? Was the whore a pretty one?"

"You seen any commotion in town this morning?" Smith asked. "Any strangers coming through?"

"Commotion every morning, no strangers," the lawman said. "But I been drunk."

Clint saw it was useless trying to talk to this man and walked out. On the street, a few people had gathered to gawk at the front of the sheriff's office. Word had probably spread that strangers were in town, and Bloody Spur didn't look like it saw many newcomers.

"We're looking for two men," Clint said. "Redheaded fella and one with black hair. They would have rode in this morning, looking for food, water, maybe fresh horses."

The five or six men, miners mostly, stared back at Clint blankly.

"Anybody see any strangers in town?" Clint asked.

"Seen you," one of the miners answered. "And your friends."

Spotting Witt and Kendal across the street, Clint walked toward them. DeGraw was missing, vanished somewhere among the shacks and shanties.

"You hear anything?" Clint asked Witt and Kendal.

"You talk to these people, they don't say nothing," Witt answered. "Something must be wrong with the whole lot of them."

"Hard luck is what's wrong with 'em," DeGraw said, from behind Clint. "I been asking around, nobody saw nothing."

"Well, they got no reason to lie," Clint said, looking toward the five or six men still gathered in front of the sheriff's office.

As Clint was watching the office, Smith came out shaking his head, followed by the other sheriff, who stumbled hesitantly into the light the way someone who doesn't know how to swim steps into a stream.

"I don't think they came through," the sheriff said. "And I want to tell you, I'd be lyin' if I said I blamed them."

EIGHT

The five of them stood in the center of the street, quietly discussing a plan as the crowd in front of the sheriff's office grew. It was rare when strangers rode into Bloody Spur, and even more rare when they didn't leave just as quick. Five men standing in the middle of the street talking was something of a novelty.

They were still discussing their options when the woman ran into town. She was wearing a shabby dress, her hair flying out behind her when the men saw her.

"They killed him!" she screamed. "They came in and killed him!"

The posse turned at her approach, Clint breaking away from the group to meet the woman as she entered the street between two canvas lean-tos filled with broken barrels.

"Who killed who?" Clint asked.

"Got to get the sheriff. Where's Clyde at?" she said, trying to run past Clint.

Clint stopped her, blocking the woman's path. "Who died?" he said.

"Nobody just died, they killed him!" she screamed. "Found him up in the shack. Damn him, where's Clyde?"

She broke away then, ran past him across the street into the sheriff's office. Clint and the other men followed. When they came into the office, they found the woman trying to wake the lawman by slapping at his face and screaming in his ear. What was left of the bottle was on his desk.

"Drunk again," Smith said, seeing the hard work of sobering up the sheriff come to nothing.

"Sheriff, you get up now, you get up!" the woman screamed, slapping Clyde's face viciously. "They killed Dwight. Get up. We got to go. Dwight's dead. We got to go."

"Dwight's dead?" the sheriff said, raising his head up off the desk. "Dead?"

"Yes! Dead. Dwight's dead," she screamed, a glimmer of hope coming into her voice.

"Damn, that's a damn shame," the sheriff answered, then slumped back on his desk.

The Wells Fargo man came into the office then and stood in the doorway. "What's the commotion?" he asked.

"Dwight—somebody killed him," the girl said,

turning now to the clerk. "We got to sober Clyde up."

"Probably won't do any good," the clerk answered. "These gentlemen here just tried. By the looks of things, it seems they weren't all that successful."

The woman turned toward the posse, a question on her face that didn't make it to her mouth.

"How many men were there?" Clint asked. "Did you see them?"

"Didn't see," she said. "Two horses. I saw the tracks outside the cabin."

"Show us," Sheriff Smith said.

"We got to get Clyde up, got to," she said.

"Ma'am, Clyde won't be getting up anytime soon," Clint said. "We're looking for two men, they might have come this way."

She stared then, her eyes going from Clint to Sheriff Smith, to Kendal to DeGraw, and finally to Witt. "Who are you?" she asked. "You the law?"

"We're a posse, ma'am, out of Elsinore," DeGraw said. "You want to show us what happened and where?"

The woman, figuring a sober posse was better than a drunk sheriff, nodded somberly and went out the door. They left Witt behind to watch the horses as the rest followed the woman up a small hill and into the trees.

It was rocky ground on a steep incline. They had to move slow. When they reached the top of the hill, she turned north on a small trail. A half mile down the trail, they came to a stream and she followed alongside, the men at her back. She started climbing up the hill again until it leveled off into a clearing. There was a rude cabin. A man lay facedown in the dirt at its door, a scattergun just out of his reach.

"See, they killed him," she said, pointing from the edge of the clearing. "Shot him like a dog."

Clint and the sheriff moved forward toward the body. The man was so skinny he looked half-starved. When they turned him over, the ground under the body was soaked with blood. There were two bullet holes in his chest.

"Think it's her husband?" Clint asked in a whisper.

"Likely," the sheriff said, rising back up.

They walked back to the woman, who was standing there chewing at her thumb. Not crying, but nervous.

"Was he your husband, ma'am?" the sheriff asked, taking off his hat in a show of respect.

"Husband died six months ago," she said. "He was helping me work the claim."

Clint walked back to the body, picked up the scattergun, and broke it open. Two shells, unfired.

"You hear the shots?" Clint asked.

"Heard 'em. I thought he was hunting rabbit," she said. "I kept at the creek. When I came down, I found him and ran to town."

"How long ago?"

"The shots? I don't know, this morning, before noon."

The woman's eyes watched Clint handle the gun. "We saw some rabbit this morning. He came back for the gun. I kept working the sluice."

THE POSSE FROM ELSINORE 71

"Sheriff," Clint said, pointing down toward where the lawman was standing. Smith looked down and saw the tracks. Two sets of prints. Then a man's set where one of them got down off his horse. The boot tracks led to the body, the scattergun, and the cabin.

The story was easy to piece together. The man came out of the cabin with the shotgun as the two outlaws rode up. They saw the gun and shot him. One got down off his horse, walked to the corpse, and kicked the gun away. The other held the horses while his partner went into the cabin looking for supplies.

Clint and the sheriff sent the others looking for the trail and took the woman into the cabin and sat her down. Inside it was shabbier than on the outside. A bed, a small Prairie Queen stove, table, chairs, and washbasin.

They didn't have to ask if anything was missing. The outlaw had made a mess of the place, spilling cornmeal and flour across the dirt floor. A wood crate that served as the larder was tipped, spilling out a quantity of salted meat. The outlaw hadn't even bothered looking for anything of value. But all it would take was a quick glance around the small shack to know these people had nothing of value.

"Oh, Lord, he died for cornmeal," she said. "He would have given it to them, he was like that. Always givin' strangers things. They could have rode up and asked him for some."

"More than likely they saw the gun, ma'am," Clint said. "They rode up and saw him with the gun and shot him."

She seemed to consider this for a long time before saying anything else. "He wasn't a bad sort," she said at last. "After my husband died, we worked the claim together. He wasn't a bad sort. Hard worker."

"Yes, ma'am," the sheriff said.

"You say you're looking for these fellas?" she asked, her eyes still dry.

"We're looking for them," Clint said. "They tried to rob a stage in Elsinore and killed some people."

"And now they killed one more, didn't they?"

"Yes, ma'am," Clint answered.

"Then we best get him in the ground," she said, standing up.

"There a preacher or someone we can call on for the burying?" the sheriff asked.

"No preacher in hell," the woman said bitterly. "That's just what this place is."

It took them the better part of two hours to dig the grave in the rocky soil. The woman sat nearby on a rock and watched with a face that told Clint she was deep in thought.

When they had the body wrapped in a blanket and in the hole, the men gathered around for the sheriff to say a few words.

"This ain't a happy thing we're doing here," the lawman said. "Not happy, not pleasant at all. I guess your life was a hard one, friend. And I hope whatever you find is better."

Then they began shoveling the dirt back into the hole and marked it with a couple of barrel staves tied together with rawhide.

"It wasn't much, but it was the best we could do,"

the lawman said as they gathered around the grave.

"More than he probably expected," the woman said, looking down. "Where'd you say you were heading?"

"Reno, ma'am," the sheriff answered. "We'll get them fellas, count on it."

"I'm going with you, that's what I'm counting on," she said.

The sheriff started to say something, but DeGraw hushed him. Then the men excused themselves into a circle to discuss the matter.

"We can't have her going along," Kendal said. "Slow us down."

"Well, we can't leave her here," Clint said.

"She'll find another man," Kendal answered. "Hell, she did it once, she can do it again."

"We're taking her," DeGraw put in. "Take her as far as the next town."

"They're putting miles between us and them," the sheriff said. "You know that."

"They're heading north, we know that for a fact," DeGraw said. "They're more than likely riding for Reno. They don't have any more money in their poke than they did when they lit out from Elsinore. They got some food is all."

"What do you think?" the sheriff asked Clint.

"I think DeGraw here is right," Clint answered. "When they reach Reno or Candelaria, someplace where there's something to buy, they're gonna want something to spend."

"I was thinking that, too," the lawman said. "More than likely they rode through Bloody Spur.

Saw there wasn't anything to steal and went up in the hills looking for food. They're gonna try again, maybe not a stage. But they'll try."

"That's what I'm saying," Kendal protested. "We ride hard, we can catch 'em. Take her, we'll fall behind more. It's gonna be just that much harder with her riding along."

The sheriff thought on this for a long time. "You got yourself a good opinion there, son," the lawman said, addressing Kendal. "But I'll be damned if I'm gonna leave her here. We take her with us."

The men went back and approached the woman, who had retaken her position on the rock. She looked at them hopefully.

"You can go," the sheriff said. "You can go as far as the next stage stop. Get your things."

"There ain't nothing I want in there," she said.

"Get yourself a bedroll," Clint advised. "You'll need it."

The woman disappeared into the cabin and almost immediately came out carrying a rolled blanket.

"No other dress or anything?" Clint asked.

"I'm wearing the only one I got," she said in a small voice.

They walked back into town to find Witt sitting on a broken barrel, a crowd of small children forming a loose circle around him. He wasn't paying them any mind as they stared at him like they would some strange animal who decided to walk in out of the trees and sit himself down. The way they looked at him, Clint saw, it was a wonder one of the braver children hadn't decided to poke the young man in relatively clean clothes with a stick.

"Damn, what took you so long?" Witt asked, jumping up to greet the others.

"Had to bury a fella," Clint told him.

"This came, Wells Fargo fella brought it to me," Witt said, holding out a folded piece of paper.

The sheriff took the note, unfolded it, and began reading, his lips moving slightly.

"What is it?" Kendal asked.

"Wells Fargo office in San Francisco," the sheriff said. "They heard about the robbery in Elsinore already. Offering five thousand reward for the two men."

"Hot damn, they're gonna give us five thousand?" Kendal said.

"This telegraph wasn't just to us," the sheriff said. "It was to Clyde in there. They went and telegraphed every lawman between Elsinore and Reno."

Clint knew immediately what that meant. And judging from the look on the sheriff's face, he knew what it meant, too. It meant that every dry-gulcher, regulator, and bounty hunter who walked into a lawman's office would see the notice. The posters would be spread by stage. The Wells Fargo office was sending out an invite.

NINE

To everyone's surprise, the woman had a small poke of gold dust. It wasn't much, but it was enough to buy her a sad-looking horse and saddle. The horse was an old swaybacked beast with gummy eyes and a weary put-upon look on its face. The saddle was dry-rotted away to such a degree that when Clint slapped it up on the beast, a fine red-brown leather dust rose from it.

The men pretended not to notice.

It was almost dusk by the time they finally pointed their horses out of town. In any other place they might have considered spending the night, but not Bloody Spur. An hour or even a minute longer in that godforsaken place was too long.

As they reached the trail north, the sheriff took up a position in front, his eyes down on the side of the trail looking for tracks where the outlaws might have reentered. Kendal, Witt, and DeGraw rode three abreast just behind the lawman, talking quietly amongst themselves. Next came Clint and the girl. He rode slowly, letting his horse keep pace with the sorry critter she rode.

Clint kept his mouth shut for a few miles, figuring on letting the woman be alone with her thoughts. They were maybe five miles outside of town when she started speaking.

"I'm just another hard luck story to you fellas, aren't I?" she asked.

"I wouldn't say that," Clint answered. "Everybody has their share. There's enough to go around."

"I must have gotten seconds, then," she answered. "Lord knows where I asked for it, but I got more than my share."

"It goes like that, sometimes."

"It wasn't always like this," she said. "Wasn't always this bad."

"I don't suppose it was," Clint answered, his eyes fixed straight ahead.

"Came out from Philadelphia," she said. "Wanted to see the West. I wouldn't be lying to you if I said I've seen just about all I can stand."

"Towns like that, they aren't kind to women," Clint answered. "It's a tough life, even if you're lucky."

"Luck's just a rumor to me, Mr. Adams," she answered. "You or the others haven't even asked my name."

"I was wondering what it might be."

THE POSSE FROM ELSINORE 79

"Stop thinking on it, it's Mary," she said. "Mary Clanahan. That was my married name, anyways. I figure I'll keep it. Only damned thing he ever gave me anyway."

Clint chuckled and turned to her. "You got any kind of plan, about what you want to do next?"

"Thinking of maybe getting a respectable job in a respectable town," she said. "Save enough to go back East. Start again where I started the first time."

"That sounds like a plan," Clint said. "Pretty girl like you shouldn't have any trouble."

"Save your flattery, Mr. Adams," she said. "I know what I look like. I been digging in dirt and sluicing a stream for two years. But I ain't been away from mirrors that long."

Then the sheriff raised his hand, pulling up his horse to a stop. Clint nodded his apology to the woman and rode up to where the other men had gathered in a loose circle.

"Looks like they came through here, somebody did," the sheriff said.

The foliage around the side of the road was trampled down, and a set of two new tracks led onto the road.

The woman had joined the loose circle. She looked down with a shrewd appraisal. "That's them," she said at last. "That's them."

"You sure of that?" the sheriff asked.

She nodded, still staring at the ground. "An Indian trail about a half mile up through there leads to the cabin. This around here is where it heads off east. If they wanted to get north, they would have had to come down around here."

The sheriff studied the sun, which was heading down behind the trees. Two more hours of light. And the outlaws were still less than a day's ride ahead of them.

The lawman spurred his horse on and they continued on the trail. They wouldn't make the next town by nightfall, but they would sometime the next day. Maybe mid-afternoon, if the woman's horse didn't do anything foolish, such as die on her. If the horse lasted until the next town of any consequence, they'd be free of her.

"I don't mind telling you, that's a lot of money," Kendal said. "Five thousand, split five ways. Still a lot of money."

"Just like those Wells Fargo bastards, though," the sheriff said. "Saved them ten thousand, they offer five. Ain't that just like them."

"They got to make a profit, too," Kendal said. "I won't deny them that."

"They got to make a profit, sure," the sheriff replied. "It's just interesting to know the price they put on an employee's life. Damned if I'd ever work for them, knowing my life wasn't worth more than five thousand."

Clint had to admit the sheriff had a point there, but he kept his mouth closed. When money entered into anything, it changed it, or rather it changed the people around it.

"I could set myself up for a thousand," Witt said.

"Fine clothes, my own store. That would be something."

It was late and the fire was burning low. The men and the woman were sitting close around it, enjoying its last warmth before turning in for the night.

"We haven't got it yet, boys," the sheriff said. "By now every two-bit dry-gulcher has already saddled up and started riding. And they're all thinking the same thing. Thinking about just how much money a five-thousand-dollar bounty is."

"True, but a thousand is still a pleasant prospect," DeGraw said, smoking a cigar. "Gives this whole enterprise a different flavor, as it were."

With DeGraw's words, Clint thought, Now we're going to see what stuff these men are really made of.

Clint awoke to the sound of screaming. The scream pulled him out of his sleep into the gray dawn. A moment later, he had grabbed his gun from the holster near his head and was running into the trees toward the sound.

It was the woman, he knew it before he was even fully awake. Her voice distorted by the scream but still her own. As he ran, he thought of what trouble, what possible problem could have caused her to cry out.

Behind him, Clint heard the sound of trampling brush as the others followed. A quarter mile into the trees he saw her. Or rather he saw her back as a large man held a shotgun to her.

The man appeared to be almost a giant, well over six feet tall, in a black oilskin and black shirt. He had a large head made larger by a solid black beard streaked with gray.

"Let's all settle down here 'fore someone gets hurt," the man said, though he didn't lower the shotgun.

"Let 'er go," Clint demanded.

"I ain't holding her," came the answer. "She can go."

"Lower that scattergun, toss it over here," Clint ordered.

"Well, now, that's a different proposition altogether, ain't it?"

The others had come up behind Clint, their guns drawn down on the stranger.

"I count five of you, five," the big man said, moving the scattergun a little from Clint toward the others.

"That's right," Clint said. "Five and the woman."

Clint saw now what had happened. A small pile of deadfall branches lay at the woman's feet. She had gotten up to gather wood for the morning fire and come across the stranger. "Walk back this way," he said to her.

She took a tentative step back, waiting for the stranger to fire at her. When he didn't, she took another step, and another, until she was behind Clint surrounded by the others.

"See, free to go," the stranger said. "Free as a damned bird. Fly away, pretty lady. Go 'head, just go on and fly yourself out of here."

"Who are you?" Clint asked.

"That's a sensible question," the big man said. "Name's Doran, Ashford Doran."

"And why'd you pull down on her?" the sheriff asked, behind Clint.

"Smelled your fire last night," Doran said. "Decided to have a look-see this morning. My camp's up a little ways."

"What's your business out here, Mr. Doran?" the sheriff said.

The big man smiled, lifted the scattergun, and scratched his bearded chin with the barrels. "I do believe, if that drunken lawman in Bloody Spur is right, it's the same as your business. Looking for a couple of hard cases. They robbed the Wells Fargo stage a few days back in Elsinore, killed a man at Bloody Spur."

"Bounty hunter, are you?" Clint said.

"I been called worse by worse than you I suppose," Doran answered.

"We're the Elsinore posse, Mr. Doran, so you can just pack up and go home," Witt said. "We got them. They're our outlaws."

Doran smiled again. "Son, you don't know what you got," he said. "I was tracking those boys a week before they rode into Elsinore. Been tracking them since they robbed the S&P down around Ukia. Now that the reward is up to five thousand, I don't aim to leave off, just so the Elsinore posse can collect the money from the Wells Fargo office."

"You care to prove that?" Kendal asked.

Doran smiled again, reached into his coat, and pulled out a wanted poster. A flick of his wrist opened it. The poster showed a crude drawing of three men, including the one that had died in Elsinore. It was offering a thousand-dollar reward for their capture. "Like I said, I been tracking those old boys before they set foot in Elsinore," he said. "By rights, you men are hunting my game."

"They shot my man, killed him," the woman said. "Killed him like a damned dog."

"I'm sorry to hear that," Doran said, returning the poster to his pocket. "But seeing how you're not offering money for justice, I don't see where that matters to me."

Clint put his gun away, tucking it into the belt, outlaw style. "Your camp's behind you, north?"

"Came down an Indian trail," Doran said. "Fastest way. I figured I'd get to where they're heading before they do. Welcome them, so to speak."

What Doran said made sense to Clint.

"We're going to be moving along now, Mr. Doran," the sheriff said finally. "We're not looking for trouble."

"Neither am I, Sheriff," the bounty hunter answered. "But I ain't backing away either. You understand me, don't you? Six thousand dollars. For me to back away from six thousand, it's gonna take a whole lot more trouble than you folks can provide."

The men backed off, keeping the woman close by. When they reached their camp, Kendal said, "Hot damn, *six* thousand."

"What do you think, Mr. Adams?" the sheriff asked, hunching down by the fire.

Clint thought on it for a moment. "I think he reached Elsinore after the shooting and somebody told him about us. Then he reached Bloody Spur a little after we all left. He hasn't been tracking the men. He's been tracking us hoping we'll lead him to the men. She just surprised him in the trees is all.''

"I was thinking the same thing," the sheriff said. "Damn lucky we didn't catch 'em. Lucky for us."

"Why's that, Sheriff?" Witt asked. "We'd have more than a thousand each in our pockets. S&P and Wells Fargo money."

" 'Cause he would have killed us in our sleep if we had those men," DeGraw answered. "That name, I heard of him. Doran. Supposed to be a mean son of a bitch."

"I don't doubt it," the lawman answered. "Man like that, working alone. I bet he is mean."

"Come on, we'll get moving before he gets too much of a lead on us," Clint said.

TEN

"I'll tell you the first thing, I ain't sharing no reward with that son of a bitch," Kendal said. "Six thousand divided up five ways is just fine with me and I don't plan on taking less."

"That's if we get them, son," the sheriff said. "Only if we get them."

"We'll get them," Witt offered. "We'll get those six-thousand-dollar bastards."

They'd been riding maybe two hours, and Kendal, Witt, and DeGraw could talk of nothing but the reward. The money. Just the idea of the money—six thousand dollars—was enough to keep them moving their mouths. They spoke the number at every chance, like they were saying a prayer. The sheriff, for his part, kept quiet. And Clint hoped it was because he was an honest man, not because of some other problem.

"I was thinking, you know," Witt said. "If they're heading for Candelaria. If they do something there, the reward is going to go up. Maybe if we wait a day they'll be worth ten thousand. Wouldn't that be something?"

Nobody made to answer.

"Well, wouldn't it?" Witt said. "Mr. Adams, wouldn't that be something? Ten thousand. We double our money by waiting a day to arrest them."

"Son, maybe you should keep quiet for now," Clint suggested.

"That's fine for you, Mr. Adams," the boy said. "You ain't been sweeping out a store, measuring flour, and cutting material for two years. My share—two thousand dollars—I get that and I can walk out of the store, forever."

"And do what, son?" the sheriff asked. "Two thousand is a lot of money, but it isn't a lifetime's worth."

"Maybe buy my own store and hire some poor bastard to do the sweeping and measuring," Witt said. "Maybe go to San Francisco. Go to the biggest, nicest hotel and smoke cigars. Sit around like a gentleman in a nice suit with a gold watch. I'd like that for once in my damned life. If I never do nothing else, I could say I did that."

"You're talking like a fool, son," DeGraw said. "Just a pure fool."

"Maybe become a bounty hunter myself then," Witt said. "Follow criminals and outlaws and such.

This ain't so bad. Better than sweeping."

"It's starting," the sheriff whispered to Clint. "I seen this before."

"Me, too," Clint said. "It's the money."

"It's the money," the sheriff agreed, then spurred his horse forward.

They reached Candelaria by noon. It was a proper town, built around a proper silver mine. The railroad ran into its center. The hotel was constructed of brick, and signs on the town's five saloons advertised "French Champagne" and "Fresh Oysters."

"Not so far away, was it?" Mary said as they rode into town. "Back in Bloody Spur it was like the moon. Far away as the moon."

Clint nodded, watching the streets bustling with activity of horses and wagons.

They gave the horses to Witt to take to the livery and the rest of them headed for the hotel. First thing, Mary ordered herself a bath. Clint followed the others out onto the street. After a brief discussion, there was a general opinion that the outlaws would head for a saloon and that might prove the best place to find them. But even if they hadn't headed for a saloon, that would certainly also prove the best place to find a drink after a long ride.

Clint put down two whiskeys quick and excused himself. He was weary of the talk of reward money, weary of the other men's company.

"If you find them, you come back now," DeGraw said. "Take them alone or with us, we still split the reward."

"Damn right," Witt added, downing his whiskey. "We rode into this town together, we're riding out with the reward in all our pockets."

Clint ignored them as he walked through the saloon doors into sunlight. He knew what he was looking for, and after a few inquiries he found the right store.

An hour later, Clint was standing in front of Mary's door with a packet. He knocked and she called, "Who is it?"

"It's me," Clint said. "I brought you something. I'm leaving it by the door."

The waiter was just putting down the plate with the steak on it when she walked into the small hotel dining room. For a brief instant, Clint couldn't believe his own eyes. The dress he'd left for her wasn't anything special, just a plain gingham, the kind ranchers' wives wore. But she filled out the dress nicely. More than nicely in fact. As she entered the room, every man in it stopped, forks halfway to their mouths, and stared.

With the new dress, the bath, and her hair done up like she had it, Mary looked a full ten years younger. She was a beauty to match any woman he'd seen in a long time.

"You like it?" she asked, spinning girlishly in front of the table.

"I like it," Clint said.

"I told you I didn't always look like that," she said.

The waiter pulled out a chair for her and she took a seat at Clint's table.

THE POSSE FROM ELSINORE

"I believed you," he answered, still a little shocked by the transformation.

"No, you didn't," she said, giggling.

"Well, I do now," he replied. "I sure as hell do now. If you told me the world was an orange I'd believe you."

She giggled again.

Clint ordered champagne and steak and tried not to stare at the way her ample breasts filled out the material of the dress.

They ate slowly, enjoying one another's company. She drank the champagne as if it were some magic elixir, cradling the glass in two hands.

"I want to show you something in my room," she said when they were almost finished with their meal.

"And what would that be?" he replied.

"Me," she said, and giggled again.

When they reached her room, he went in first, then she shut the door, as if trapping him. Her back against the door, she held the key in her hand.

"Are you ready for your reward now, Mr. Adams?" she asked, smiling. The girlish giggle was now replaced by a woman's smile of mischief.

"Reward?" he answered, playing along.

"For rescuing me," she said, and began unbuttoning the small white buttons that ran up the front of the dress.

When all of the buttons were undone, she opened the dress and brought it down slowly off her shoulders. She wore very little beneath it.

"Do you like what you see?" she asked, walking toward him slowly. "Do you?"

"I confess I do," he said.

"Anything you want," she whispered. "Anything."

Clint walked the two steps toward her and gathered her up into his arms. He could feel her softness trembling with desire in his arms.

Lowering his head, he kissed her, their tongues meeting between their locked lips.

When they broke off the kiss after a long time, he took a half step back and brought his hands up to fiddle with the strings that secured her underclothes.

She had tied the top strings in tight little bows, and it took him a moment to pull them free. Then, with the final pull of the string, her breasts came free and he eased the garment down over her smooth, white shoulders.

Her breasts were magnificent, large and firm with pink nipples. He lowered his head to her breasts and let his tongue play around the nipples.

"Oh, Mr. Adams," she whispered, arching her back to his ministrations. "Clint. Oh, that feels so wonderful."

He felt one nipple hardening under his teasing tongue, then moved his head to tend to the other. As he worked on her breasts, standing there in the middle of the room, he felt her hand slide seductively up the front of his pants to rest on his hard, throbbing member.

When both nipples were hardened with excitement, he stepped back again and slowly began peeling off the remainder of her undergarments. He pulled the material down slowly, planting small teasing kisses on each inch of skin he exposed.

Finally, when she was completely naked, he sat on the bed and began running his tongue down her smooth, white belly.

Her body continued trembling, the knees slightly buckling, coming together with his kisses and small teasing jabs of his tongue, until he had reached her silken nest.

With the first touch of his tongue on her already moist thatch, she let out another long, low moan.

Sitting on the bed with Mary standing before him, he ran his tongue up the inside of first one silken thigh and then another. Each time he ended his short teasing route at the top of her thatch.

She opened her legs wider, urging him in, begging him to enter her moist secret place. But Clint held off for what seemed like hours as wave after wave of pleasure washed over her.

Finally, when he himself could take it no longer, he fell back across the bed, her on top of him. She scrambled up on her knees quickly, greedily working at his belt, his pants, seeking to free the hard shaft that would provide even more pleasure.

When the shaft sprang free, she spread her legs wide and lowered herself on it, taking him in all at once in a single long stroke.

"Oh, Clint, that feels, that feels so good," she said. "I've never . . . never . . ."

Slowly Clint began moving his hips up off the bed as she ground herself down on him. Reaching up with both hands, he cupped her breasts, then began teasing the nipples again with his thumbs, brushing them first one way, then the other.

He could feel her trembling more intensely with each stroke in and out of her. Clint raised his hips high to meet each of her movements.

When she was close, she fell forward toward him, her breasts pressed against his chest, her mouth desperately seeking his mouth.

He grabbed her tightly around the waist, drawing her closer down on him as he released inside of her.

"That, that was, oh, so good," she said. "So nice."

Clint opened his eyes and smiled up at her as she slid off of him. Her face was flushed, very nearly glowing with pleasure.

One of her hands came down and took his slick shaft between her small fingers. She began stroking him idly. And very soon he was hard again.

"This way, please," she said, getting up on her hands and knees. "From behind."

Clint arranged himself behind her. She reached around and guided him into her warmth for the second time.

Then she was moving under him, her hips wriggling back and forth as she knelt forward on the bed.

Clint reached around and cupped one of her breasts as she let out a long, low moan.

ELEVEN

Clint left Mary's bed the next morning and joined the others down in the hotel's small dining room. Before he even entered the room, he saw that the mood around the table was grim.

"Lost twenty dollars at poker last night," Witt said. "Damn, if I wasn't going to be rich as hell real soon, that would bother me."

Clint could tell it bothered him just the same but said nothing. Twenty dollars was a good piece of money to a boy like Witt. To lose it all in a few minutes at a saloon card game had to have hurt his pride and his wallet both.

A waiter put a cup of coffee in front of Clint and he sipped at it. Across the way, three men in fine suits sat talking in hushed, confidential tones. Clint took them for bankers, local businessmen.

"How do you get like that?" Witt asked, indicating the three men. "How you figure they got like that? Those fine suits and all."

"Not by trying to fill an inside straight against three queens," the sheriff answered glumly and dug into his eggs with a knife and fork.

"Upshot is, we didn't see nothing of them in town last night," DeGraw said.

"And you boys searched pretty good, didn't you?" the sheriff said. "I turned in after the third saloon, but you boys had what you might call dedication to the job at hand. Something to admire."

"We looked, didn't we?" Kendal answered sharply. "Damn it, we looked."

"Looked through the bottom of beer glasses," the sheriff grumbled.

"Where else but a saloon you expect to find those critters?" Kendal asked. "You tell me that, Sheriff. Where do you expect us to look?"

"Did you talk to the law in town?" Clint asked, taking another sip from the hot coffee. It wasn't much of a question, but it was the most sensible thing he could think to ask.

"Did," the sheriff answered, chewing his eggs slowly. "Half the town is strangers to him. He won't see 'em unless they break the law. But I'll tell you this, we ain't the only ones looking. That dodger is out from here to hell and back. There's a pack of folks looking for those old boys."

"Looking for our money, you mean," Kendal spat. "Looking for a chance to take the credit for bringing them in to their justice."

The waiter brought more food, and the men dug into it, eating silently, each lost in his own thoughts.

For Clint's part, he was trying to think of a reason why he shouldn't just get up and ride out of town. Shake their hands while he still could and keep heading north. The whole enterprise was turning ugly. He could see where it would be leading but felt helpless to stop it.

"Know what I was thinking last night?" DeGraw said, leaning back in his chair.

Nobody answered; they just stared at their plates of half-eaten food.

"I was thinking—just thinking of it, mind you—what a fine thing it would be to own a saloon," he said. "A big place for gentlemen."

"Elsinore's got a saloon," the sheriff said. "Damn fine one, too."

"Not in Elsinore," DeGraw said, tilting his chair back. "Place like this, maybe. A town where they can appreciate some of the finer things."

"That right?" Kendal asked.

"I took a notion last night, started watching the barkeeps," DeGraw explained. "In its own way, a saloon, a good one, is a thing of true and lasting beauty, if you catch my meaning. Like I said, I noticed it last night, watching the barkeeps."

"Watched and kept them busy, both," the sheriff replied drily as he shoveled more egg into his mouth.

"I'm watching the barkeeps," DeGraw continued, unmoved by the lawman's criticism, "and I'm thinking, what a fine thing when what you're selling comes in a bottle. I'm thinking, what a fine thing that when after you've sold it you're left with nothing but money. I'm saying that now, as opposed to my current line of merchandise."

Clint noticed that DeGraw's full attention was aimed at Witt. He pointed his words directly at the boy, the way some men might point a gun.

"You're thinking of selling the house?" Witt asked. "Moving on?"

"That I am," DeGraw said expansively. "I figure I'm getting a little too old for it. Not that there aren't benefits to the work, mind you. Being a respected member of the community . . ."

"You own a whorehouse, DeGraw," the sheriff spat. "You ain't mayor or judge, and you certainly ain't any doctor or preacher."

". . . fine clothes and such like that," DeGraw continued. "And I'll admit it, there is the benefit that I'll use my own products from time to time. If you catch my drift."

"Damn, how much you looking to get for it?" the boy said, leaning over the table, truly interested in what could possibly be a future business venture, seeing as he was soon to be rich in his own right.

DeGraw shrugged. "I haven't given it that much thought," he said. "Just occurred to me last night while we were looking for those fellas."

"Leave the boy alone, DeGraw," the sheriff warned. "He don't need no part of a cathouse."

"Sheriff, I don't see any boy here," DeGraw answered. "I see a man. Witt here, he's every bit a man. Just that nobody let him prove it before. What with making him wear that apron and all. But now I see it. I've seen it on this little adventure of ours.''

"Damn right," Witt said, almost bursting. "How much you figuring on getting for it?"

"You got to figure that when you got a business like that, you own something that will put money in your pocket and clothes on your back for the rest of your life," DeGraw said. As if to further illustrate the point, he drew a cigar from his pocket and cut the end with a solid gold pocketknife. "Yes, sir, it's a fine business."

What DeGraw didn't say, but what Clint knew, was that when anyone had a business like that, he ran the risk of watching his "merchandise" leave on any stage or rail that came to town. Not to mention leave with any ten-dollar-a-week cowpoke with a smooth flow of words.

"How much?" the boy asked, bursting now. "If you're talking serious, serious business, you might as well name a price."

Clint watched and felt a sickness rising up in him. The boy was clearly no match for DeGraw. There was not even any talk directly of Witt buying the whorehouse, yet it was understood by all that he was the customer. DeGraw had hooked him like a prize fish. All that was left to be done was reel him in and gut him.

"I'm talking about selling to a fella with some business sense," DeGraw said. "And some lady sense, if you catch my meaning. The fella that I sell to is going to have to be smart. And I don't mean book smart, neither."

Clint could see what would happen if the boy

bought it. Like looking into the future. The girls would steal enough to leave for bigger cities. The customers wouldn't pay the asking price. Witt would spend freely, squandering money on cards and liquor and clothes. The entire business would end in disgrace. If the boy lasted a year in such a business it would be some kind of miracle. The boy lacked that particular brand of charming viciousness needed to run such an operation in Elsinore or anywhere else. Inside of six months, Witt would be back sweeping shops in his new set of mail-order clothes. Clint had no doubt that DeGraw could see this sad and sorry fate as well. He could see it and was doing his best to lure him into it.

"How much?" the boy asked, leaning now across the table anxiously.

"Leave 'im alone, DeGraw," the sheriff said. "Stop it, and I mean now."

"Just talking, Sheriff," DeGraw answered. "No law against that, is there? When it's against the law for two men to talk business, well, then, that's a sorry damned day for all concerned."

"That kind of talk should be against some law," the sheriff said disgustedly, then got up from the table and left the room.

DeGraw was waiting for that moment. As soon as the sheriff was out of earshot, he leaned across the table and said, "I'd be willing to part with my business for two thousand dollars in cash."

The number sat the boy back down in his seat as neatly as if DeGraw had punched him between the eyes. "Two thousand, damn," he said, suddenly aware that DeGraw's talk might not have been aimed at him, but rather someone else, someone who had two thousand in their pockets.

"A bargain, a genuine bargain at two thousand," DeGraw said.

"I won't have that much even after we catch them bastards," Witt said. "That's a lot of damned money for anyone in Elsinore."

"Well, I was just talking," DeGraw said. "Just talk is all."

Clint watched as DeGraw tilted his chair back into place and rose from the table. "Gentlemen," he said, touching a finger to his hat.

Clint pushed his chair back and followed him out onto the boards. "Why do that to the boy?" Clint asked. "Hold something like that in front of him?"

DeGraw was standing on the boards, looking out over the busy street. The cigar was clamped between his teeth, a fine cloud of blue-gray smoke trailing off behind him.

Clint noticed then that in the light of day there was a hardness about him.

"Friend, I don't know what you're talking about," he said. "Me and the boy was having a little talk is all. Discussing business."

"Talk like that is going to get that boy killed," Clint said, coming up alongside DeGraw. "Maybe get one of us killed if we tried to help him."

"I don't plan on dying anytime soon," DeGraw said. "You tell me now if you got any particular plans in that direction. Give me some warning not to stand too close when you feel the time might be near."

Clint stared at him, not speaking, knowing there was a special place in hell for people like DeGraw.

"What Witt does is his own business," DeGraw said. "Doesn't concern me or you. I offered the boy an opportunity. Not even offered, more like to just tell him about it. But if you stuck your nose into his business, or mine, I'd feel obliged to take offense."

Away from his girls, his own town, and his home, all of DeGraw's charm had fallen away. Clint saw the whole man clearly. Maybe Kendal didn't see it, he was no more than a boy himself, but the sheriff saw it and Clint sure as hell did. And what he saw disgusted him.

Clint turned and began walking down the boards. He had gone no more than ten yards when DeGraw called out to him. Clint turned, faced the man.

"Adams, that offer goes for anyone," DeGraw said, a nasty smile spreading across his face. "Two thousand in cash and she belongs to you."

"Don't think so," Clint said.

"I'm askin' 'cause from where I stand, you got a damned better chance of laying your hands on two thousand than that boy in there," DeGraw said. "You're a man who could do it with just a little planning."

TWELVE

Clint sat in a saloon studying the poster of the two gunmen. From the crude sketches on the paper, there could be little doubt that they were the men who had tried to rob the stage in Elsinore. Their names were Vizard and Montano.

Vizard was the redheaded one; Montano, the one with the dark features. Clint looked back at the dead-eyed stare of the drawings and wondered where they could be hiding.

Clint remained so engrossed in the poster, he didn't note Mary's approach. Nor did he notice when she took a seat opposite him at the small table.

"Mr. Adams, you are going to scandalize me outright," she said, smiling across the table.

She was wearing the dress that Clint had purchased for her the day before and which he had taken off her the night before. He had to admit, she looked good. Briefly, he thought of taking her back up to the hotel room, but Witt was gathering up supplies and then the horses. They would be back on the trail within an hour.

"You're smiling," Clint said, curious.

"I have reason to smile, the first good reason in a long time," she said. "I got myself a job."

"Honest work?" Clint asked, suspicious not only of the speed with which she had found employment, but the fact that she had found it at all. Boomtowns like Candelaria were tough for even men to find work in. Even in good times, there was always more men than money.

"Honest work," she confirmed, still smiling. "General merchandise hired me to look after their lady customers. There's more than ever now that this place is becoming a proper town."

"Shop girl?" Clint asked. "That's nice."

"I'll be selling the local ladies notions and fabrics. It doesn't pay much, but I'll manage. And it's a damn way better than scraping in the ground for gold."

"That's nice, then," Clint said.

Then she noticed the poster and the smile fell from her face. "You think you'll catch them?" she asked somberly in a whisper.

"We're going to try," he said.

"That's not what I asked, Mr. Adams," she replied curtly. "I didn't ask if you'll try or if you'll keep trying. I asked if you will."

"I can't answer that," he said, meeting her steady gaze. "If they're still together there's a better than even chance. If they split up, then I can't guess."

She turned the poster around, staring at their faces. "In an odd way, I guess I have them to thank," she said. "Dwight wasn't about to leave. It was hopeless, there wasn't any gold up there, but he wasn't leaving. That hill would have killed him."

"I've seen it," Clint said. "I've seen men that get sick like that."

"And then, I wouldn't have met you," she said. "Another year, maybe two, and he would have been dead. I would have buried him and not had a friend in the world. Now I have you to thank for helping me."

"The others helped," Clint offered.

She shook her head. "Listen to me," she said in a whisper. "I wasn't going to say anything, but there's something wrong with them."

"Wrong, how?"

"I don't know," she continued. "Just wrong. I can feel it. I can feel it deep down. Watch out for that bunch. Something isn't right with this thing you've gotten yourself all mixed up in."

"I'm obliged," Clint answered, nodding, even though he didn't need her to tell him that. She was, of course, right. Something was wrong with all of them. Yet, he felt obliged to see it through.

Clint was about to say something else but was interrupted by a fuss out in the street. Shouts were coming from just beyond the doors of the saloon.

"Excuse me," he said, and made for the doors.

He found out that he was right to hurry off. Out in the center of the street, surrounded by men, were Witt and Doran. Doran was standing over the boy, who was on the ground, backing up crablike.

"You had enough, boy?" Doran said, taunting the youth. "You just speak right up when you had enough."

Witt got up, but before he could even raise his hands, Doran knocked him down again.

"You had your share, boy?" Doran said, fists up.

Witt rose and was immediately knocked back to the dirt.

Three or four more times Doran knocked Witt down, each time taunting him. And each time Witt rose slowly to take the punishment as the audience of men jeered them on.

Finally, Clint could no longer tolerate it. Lord knows, Witt probably needed a good beating, but not like this. Not in front of half a town of drunken miners.

"Doran, leave him be!" Clint ordered, coming off the boards.

The big man smiled as he turned to face Clint. "I ain't but defending myself against him."

"You defend yourself any more against him, you'll kill him," Clint said, walking to the center of the street.

"It's self-defense, they seen it," Doran said.

"I seen it, that boy asked for it," a voice from the crowd hollered.

"I seen it, too, that youngster went at him," someone else said.

"Get up," Clint ordered Witt.

The boy rose unsteadily to his feet. Oddly, he raised

his fists, as if to continue fighting. The gesture drew great bursts of laughter from the onlookers.

"This here is a private matter," Doran said.

"Get the horses," Clint told Witt.

The boy staggered first in one direction, then the other. His face was bloody and bruised with the beating. His eyes were nearly swollen shut. If he didn't feel it now, he'd feel it soon. Riding would be hard, but that was the price he'd have to pay.

"I ain't done with him, not by a long ways," Doran said, bringing his fists up.

"No, you're done," Clint said.

"You telling me my business?" Doran bellowed.

"That boy, he's my business," Clint said. "One way or the other, you're done with him."

Doran seemed to think about this for a moment, then said, "Then I ain't done with you."

Clint saw the fist coming and ducked. The big meaty fist whistled by his head. As he was bringing his head up, Clint threw a punch of his own, landing it directly into Doran's gut. It was like punching at the side of a steer.

Doran let out a gasp of air and swung again.

This blow hit Clint solid in the side, sending him staggering back down the center of the street.

Clint righted himself in time to see Doran moving in quickly, fists up in front of him.

Clint punched again, snaking a fist in between Doran's raised hands and landing on the big man's chin. The blow snapped his head back, but he swung out again.

Clint shuffled back and the blow just missed his nose.

Doran shook his head, clearing the pain, then punched out again, twice. Both blows missed, then Clint struck, landing a blow at Doran's stomach, then another across the side of his head.

Seeing that he was no match for Clint's speed, the big man charged, coming at Clint like an enraged bull. His strategy now was to use his superior weight and strength to wrestle Clint to the ground.

But before Doran could grab him, Clint let fly with another blow that struck Doran dead center in the chest, then another that caught him in the throat.

It was the second blow to the throat that sent Doran to his knees, gasping for air. Now it was Clint's turn. He stepped back, fists up, waiting. "I'm defending myself the same way you did," he said. "Come on, stand up so I can defend myself some more."

Doran raised a hand and waved it feebly in surrender.

"Listen to me, Doran, stay away from us. Stay away from the posse."

The big man, still on his knees, made no answer. Rather he just nodded.

Witt returned then, the others trailing a few steps behind.

Clint walked over to where they waited on the boards, stooping along the way to recover his hat, which had fallen off.

"Damn, boy, what did you do?" the sheriff asked.

"Taught him a lesson, I hope," Clint answered.

"Looks like you went and sent him through college and all," Kendal said.

"Son of a bitch, I've a mind to go over there and kick the tar out of him," Witt said.

"We're riding now," Clint replied. "The horses ready?"

"They're ready," Witt said without taking his swollen eyes off Doran.

THIRTEEN

They rode single file out of town, the law of Candelaria watching the progress of the five men. It wasn't a happy feeling, Clint could say that about sitting in the saddle feeling like more of an outlaw than the men he was chasing.

The sheriff of Candelaria had ordered three deputies to ride along for the first few miles, just to make certain that Clint and the posse reached the trail without any thoughts of riding back into town.

Brawling, the sheriff had explained, was forbidden in town at any time of day. But brawling in the center of the street when it wasn't even noon and none of the parties were drunk, well, that deserved special attention. That kind of meanness deserved an escort to the trail and a warning not to ride back.

This posse was not the first time Clint had helped

a lawman. But it was the first time he had helped a lawman and felt like a criminal both.

They were maybe a half mile out, heading up a narrow trail into the hills, when they heard the shots. Three shots, coming quickly, then four more. Those seven were pistol shots that echoed up at them from the town. Then came a shotgun blast.

"Damned if something isn't going on," DeGraw said, turning in his saddle.

"You just keep moving," one of the deputies ordered. "It ain't none of your concern."

There were more shots then, ringing up from the town. Now the deputies turned in their saddles. The gunfire wasn't some drunk miner firing into the air. And it wasn't a couple of drunks trying to stage a showdown over cards or a woman, either.

"This is as far as we take you," one of the deputies said, then turned his horse back toward town.

The others followed in his tracks. Clint watched as they negotiated the rocky section of trail that inclined toward the town, then spurred their animals on to a full gallop once the trail widened and flattened out some. The town lay behind a wide turn in the trail, and presently the deputies vanished around it, leaving a cloud of dust hanging in the air.

"What do you figure?" Sheriff Smith asked, pulling his horse up alongside Clint's.

"I figure that it ain't any of our business," Clint said but made no move to continue.

"Then again . . ." the sheriff answered, letting his words hang in the air like the dust from the deputies.

"Then again, it could be," Clint said.

THE POSSE FROM ELSINORE

The others held their horses back as Clint and the sheriff conferred. If it was nothing and they rode back into town, the law would have every right to toss them into a cell. If it was their men shooting up Candelaria, then their search would be over. The whole nasty business would be near the end.

"I believe there's a ridge up there," the sheriff said. "Might see something if we rode to it."

Clint nodded and turned his horse as the others followed suit. The ridge the sheriff indicated was a quarter mile down, off the main trail. By the time they reached it, more shots had been fired and shouts were rising up from the town.

As they looked out over the ridge, the town seemed normal enough, except for the lack of people on the street. The street that had bustled with the activity of horses, wagons, and people just an hour ago now stood deserted.

"Where you think they all went?" Witt asked.

"Don't know, son," the sheriff said.

Then there was another gunshot. The five men watched as a lone figure ran into the street between two buildings. His gun was out and he was firing back the way he'd come.

"Damn if that isn't Doran," Kendal said.

It was true, the figure was Doran. He was standing in the middle of the street. Then he paused, lifted his gun, and began shooting as fast as he could pull the trigger. Then he was moving again, heading back to the shelter of a doorway for cover while he reloaded.

Two more men rushed into the street from the opposite side, both with shotguns. They stopped, studying the situation, then ran down the alley Doran had run out from a few seconds before and out of sight. Two shotgun blasts sounded as a dull echo up to the ridge, then silence.

"There they are, them deputies," DeGraw said. "Bastards."

Clint watched as the three deputies and the sheriff walked down the center of the street in a ragtag line. Each held a rifle or pistol.

Something moved in one of the stores that Clint couldn't see, and the four men let loose with gunfire into the store window.

One the lawmen stopped firing. Another shot, from inside the store, echoed up and one of the lawmen fell.

"Which one they get, that skinny bastard?" Kendal asked.

The other lawmen scattered, running into stores and positioning themselves against the walls of buildings.

Doran came back out on the street, gun out, and kicked open the door to the store that the lawmen had shot up. Two more shots came from inside, sending Doran into a crouch as he aimed his gun inside without looking and fired.

"Up there, look," Clint said, pointing.

Two men emerged on the roof of the building above Doran. Both had their guns out. The deputies who were crouching in doorways and against walls didn't see the outlaws, yet they were easy targets.

"That's them!" Witt cried. "I can see 'em from here. Damn! That's them."

It was true. Clint saw clearly that it was Vizard and

THE POSSE FROM ELSINORE 115

Montano taking positions above the street.

"You gonna do something, Sheriff?" DeGraw asked. "You ain't just gonna sit here, are you?"

The sheriff pulled the Sharps from its boot and slipped a cartridge into the big gun. A moment later, he was crouching down, bracing the rifle's barrel along a rock.

"Get that redheaded bastard," Witt said.

The sheriff slowly raised the vernier sight and stared down the barrel as his finger curled around the trigger. All four men held their breath as the lawman sighted in on the outlaws.

It was a tough shot but not impossible.

One of the outlaws rose on the roof from a crouching position. He began moving, heading for the livery. Clint and the others could see the plan now. Drop down in back into the livery and retrieve their horses or steal new horses.

The sheriff tightened his finger around the trigger and fired. The big gun let off with a blast that could wake the dead. Even from their distance, the men saw the outlaw fall.

"Damn, you got him, didn't you?" Witt yelled, then let out a whoop.

"Got him nothing," DeGraw snorted, pointing to where the outlaw was getting up and starting to run across the roofs. The second outlaw nearly passed him in his own mad dash for the livery.

Doran, perhaps alerted by the large bullet slamming into the building, ran to the middle of the street and began firing up toward the roof. But the outlaws were too far back from the edge for his bullets to come close.

Now the deputies joined in, some of them running along the street with Doran, firing up at the roof.

"Damn, they don't have no chance," Kendal said. "Look at them, shooting up like a bunch of fools."

Kendal would get no argument from Clint for that comment. However, they might have been shooting up like a bunch of fools, but they were still in a position to get themselves shot as well. And Clint knew it was that kind of position that pushed men to act foolishly.

"Shoot again, Sheriff," DeGraw insisted.

"Too fast, they're moving too fast," the sheriff said, lowering the rifle.

"They're as good as got away," Witt said, tears almost coming to his eyes.

Clint started for his horse again. "We head around," he said. "If we cut 'em off at that trail behind, then we got a chance at them."

The other men, even the sheriff, didn't question the strategy. The chances of catching the two outlaws weren't good. But they were the best odds Clint could see.

A moment later they were on their horses and riding fast, following the ridge around the back side of town. The ride couldn't have lasted more than a quarter hour, yet for that time they lost sight of the town and heard only muffled shots in the distance.

Clint studied the trail, noticing a small rock ledge about twenty yards back from where the road turned down a steep incline toward town.

"Sheriff, why don't you take the high ground with Witt," Clint said. "I'll go with DeGraw down in those trees. Kendal can go down the trail, blocking their way back."

The sheriff nodded his agreement and headed for the ledge. With any luck, the outlaws would be boxed in, surrounded, the moment they rode beyond the curve in the trail.

No sooner had the five men taken up their positions than they heard the sound of horses.

Clint listened to the sound, judging it to be two riders, moving quickly. He pulled the hammer back on his pistol and waited.

The seconds stretched themselves into hours, then the two horses appeared around the corner. The men were riding low, spurring the animals furiously faster up the trail.

The sheriff brought his head up from the outcropping and fired a warning shot, kicking up dirt in front of the riders, sending the horses rearing up in panic.

"Hold it there," Clint ordered, running from the trees with DeGraw from behind the riders.

One of the riders went for his gun, and Witt nearly took Clint's head off with a shot.

Then one of the horses pinwheeled, revealing the rider's face as he struggled to gain control.

"Deputies!" Clint shouted. "It's the deputies!"

The law in Candelaria wasn't pleased. What with the mining office getting robbed of five thousand dollars, the outlaws slipping away, and two of his deputies almost getting shot by a posse, the sheriff was cursing a blue streak. It was as if he couldn't decide which piece of the long day's sorry chain of events to direct his rage at. So he aimed his anger at all of it. Obvious to all concerned was the fact that there was enough anger to go around.

Somewhere tangled up in all the cussing, Clint managed to piece together the story. What had happened was that the outlaws rode peacefully into town that morning. Stopping by one of the saloons for a beer, they chanced to look out the window to see most of the law riding five men out of town.

Not believing their good luck, the outlaws bought themselves a pair of ten-cent cigars, paused in the saloon long enough to light them and drink another beer, then headed to the mining office.

More luck awaited the outlaws in the mining office. The safe was open because it had just been filled with a new shipment of gold awaiting transport out of town.

The two clerks inside the mining office were killed immediately. So was a luckless mining foreman who chose a bad time to fill out some forms required by the company.

Everything would have gone smoothly for the two outlaws had not Doran been recovering from the beating Clint had administered. He was in a saloon, which occupied the next building. He heard the shooting and hobbled outside.

When he saw the gunmen, he started firing, but his aim wasn't what it might have been if Clint hadn't beaten him so badly.

A couple of shopkeepers came out with scatterguns,

but they didn't pose a real threat, except to store windows.

And, of course, by the time all the confusion had been settled, the outlaws were long gone.

The only real piece of genuine luck, as far as Clint could tell, was that none of the deputies had been killed by the posse. But Clint thought it neither the time nor the place to point this significant fact out to the sheriff.

FOURTEEN

They spent the night in jail while the town sheriff thought about what to do with them. He was thinking hard, anybody could see that. A full bottle of whiskey became a half bottle by small degrees throughout the night as he thought of some way to hang the posse from Elsinore.

A little before dawn the sheriff staggered back to the town's single jail cell and awoke the men by bellowing drunkenly and knocking a slop bucket against the bars.

"By God, I should hang you all," he said. "Show me the law in the book and I'll hang the lot of you in an hour."

The men kept quiet.

"But, as it is, you ain't broke no law except obstruction of justice," he continued. "That's what they tell me. And they tell me it ain't a hanging offense."

"You're gonna let us out?" Witt asked, coming up to the bars.

"You miserable vermin, I'll let you out," he said. "I don't want to, but I have to. It ain't fair. It ain't right. But it's the law."

Then the sheriff staggered back into his office and returned with the keys. "I can keep you if you can't pay the fine," he said. "Fine's ten dollars. I still can't hang you if you can't pay, but I can keep you for thirty days."

All the men could pay, and the sheriff opened the door.

By dawn they were back on the trail riding in silence.

"Almost shot a man yesterday," Sheriff Smith said, pulling his horse up alongside Clint.

"Then you did what you wanted to when you looked down that sight," Clint said, staring straight ahead.

The sheriff was silent for a long time before answering. "What's that supposed to mean, Adams?"

"It means when you pulled that rifle out you were aiming to *almost* shoot a man."

"I take offense at that, Adams," the lawman said. "I'm a sworn officer of the law. That kind of talk isn't a trifle for me."

"Not a trifle for me either, Sheriff," Clint answered. "I'm riding with a man afraid to shoot to kill a man. You think those men we're tracking are afraid? No matter what side of the law you're riding on,

THE POSSE FROM ELSINORE

thinking like you do is a dangerous thing for yourself and us."

"I didn't have the shot," the sheriff said flatly. "Didn't have it."

"It was a clean shot. It was long, but no wind. It was clean. I believe that."

"Mr. Adams, I don't give a damn what you believe," the sheriff said.

"Let me ask you something, Sheriff," Clint said. "How far was that shot where you hit the girl?"

The lawman thought. "About the same."

"In the winter, in the wind and the snow. And you took her down?"

"My bad luck," he said. "My damned bad luck."

"Sheriff, those men ain't that girl," Clint said.

"I know that, you damned fool. Don't you think I know that?" came the answer. "Let me tell you, not a day passes I don't think about her. Not a single day. They weren't bad people. They were stealing 'cause they were hungry. Hungry."

"These men, they ain't hungry, either," Clint said. "You think on that the next time."

The sheriff spurred his horse forward on the trail. Behind him, Clint could hear DeGraw talking to Witt. He was telling him of the places he'd seen and the things he'd done in his line of work.

Turning deftly in the saddle, Clint saw Witt's eyes big as saucers, his head nodding with confirmation and wonder.

"Leave 'im be, DeGraw," Clint said, turning back around in the saddle. "Just leave the boy be."

"We ain't doing nothing but talking," DeGraw answered. "Maybe you and that sheriff we just left should get together, think up a law against talking. Maybe make talking a hanging crime."

Witt chuckled at this bit of humor, and DeGraw continued with his stories. Ten, twelve miles passed with DeGraw whispering into the boy's ear the whole time. It wasn't a pleasant thing to consider, and Clint pushed it from his thoughts, concentrating instead on the killers they were tracking.

They were still heading north along the trail. But for all they knew it might have been useless. The outlaws could have very well doubled back, maybe even headed east, toward the desert and Salt Lake. There was just no way of telling.

By dusk, Clint swore he'd get on the first train depot they reached. Maybe head back to San Francisco. Maybe turn south to Labyrinth. The others, he knew, were thinking similar thoughts.

They made camp that night by a clear spring that fed into a small rock-bottomed creek with water so cold it made Clint's teeth ache.

They ate their supper in silence, each one lost in his own thoughts. Witt was particularly quiet. His thoughts had jumped beyond capturing the outlaws to owning DeGraw's whorehouse. What with DeGraw whispering in his ear mile after mile, it was easy to see the anticipation the boy felt.

Even now, sitting by the fire, DeGraw kept the boy close. He guarded the youth, protecting him from any voice other than his own, and he did this under the guise of friendship.

• • •

They had just turned in when Clint heard one of the horses snort, smelling the night air. Somewhere in the trees beyond the clearing a small stick snapped.

Rising up on his elbow, Clint pulled his Colt from the holster. Something out in the trees rustled and then it was silent.

It was a full moon or nearly so, and the trees were lit in a dull, gray light.

Then, close by, something else stirred and Witt rose from his bedroll.

Clint made a sound like a snake hissing and the boy turned toward him. "Where you going?" Clint asked.

"Water some trees," Witt answered.

In the dim light, Clint caught a glimpse of the pistol in the boy's hand as he vanished into the trees.

There was silence for a long time, then a shot.

Clint was up and out of his bedroll in a heartbeat, the gun in his hand as he rushed through the trees where the boy had vanished.

A hundred yards out, he spotted a figure. Then he smelled the gunpowder that hung in the air in a fine cloud.

"Put 'em up," Clint ordered, moving slowly toward the figure. When he got a little closer he saw the body on the ground.

The figure didn't raise his hands, but turned toward Clint. "Put 'em up!" Clint ordered again, thumbing back the hammer.

It was only when the figure was all the way turned around and Clint's finger was squeezing down on the trigger that he saw it was Witt. He was smiling.

"I got 'im," Witt said. "Shot the bastard through the heart."

Clint lowered the pistol and walked toward Witt. At his feet lay Doran.

The others arrived then, guns drawn, rushing down on them quickly.

"It's us, it's fine," Clint said.

The men gathered around the dead body. It was Doran all right and he was dead.

"Bastard's been following us again," Witt said. "I heard him out here."

"You shot him, son," the sheriff said.

"Straight through the heart," Witt said, boasting. "One shot."

"Damn, he is dead. One dead bastard," Kendal blurted out. "Damn."

"He draw down on you, son? That it?" the sheriff asked in a way that could leave no doubt what kind of answer he wanted from the boy.

Witt hesitated, taking in the sheriff's question. Finally he said, "He drew down on me."

Clint took a step forward, knelt, and turned the body over. The boy was right, the shot was through the heart. But he was lying about Doran drawing down on him. The big man's gun was still in the holster. It was his private parts not his gun that was unholstered. He had been relieving himself when Witt shot him.

"Man's got a strange fast draw," Kendal said, observing that Doran's hand was still holding his member.

THE POSSE FROM ELSINORE 127

There was, Clint noted, a look of surprise on Doran's face.

"Damn, son," the sheriff said.

Witt, sensing he was in trouble, began talking. "He was sneaking around our camp," he said. "You don't come sneaking around a camp. You announce yourself. No jury in the world would convict me."

"Except that half a town a day's ride away saw you get the tar beat out of you by him," Clint said.

"He was sneaking up," Witt insisted. "You all saw him do it before."

"Son, this isn't good," the sheriff said. "This don't look good at all."

"He was aiming to steal our money," Witt suddenly burst out. "He was aiming to capture them fellas and steal our reward money. You all know it. Hell, I done all of us a favor. Saved the reward for all of us."

Clint, standing there stunned by the outburst, could think of nothing to say. Then the sheriff grabbed him by the elbow and led him away from the body.

"We'll bury it," the lawman said.

"You gonna arrest him?" Clint asked.

"No, no I'm not."

"You're sworn to it," Clint replied. "This is murder here, no way around it."

"It's murder, but I don't care," the sheriff said. "I'm not letting that boy hang for the likes of Doran. I'd sooner go to hell myself before I let something like that happen when I could have stopped it."

"What about the others?"

"They'll go along," the sheriff said. "They've

known the boy his whole life practically. If you go along, then they will."

"And if I don't?"

"Then we got a problem," the sheriff answered. "You're forcing me outright to pick between you and him. Nobody wins that way. Doran, hell, he's dead. Hanging that poor boy won't change that."

"It's mighty convenient that way, isn't it?"

"Don't talk about convenient, not with me," the sheriff said. "Now, what's it going to be with this situation? You with us or against us?"

Clint nodded. They spent the better part of the night digging a grave for the bounty hunter. It wasn't an easy job. The ground was rocky and tightly packed. By the time they finally got him into the hole they'd dug, and covered it with stones, the first birds were singing and the sky was turning the blue-gray color of gun smoke.

They managed a few hours of sleep, and when they awoke it was as if the killing had never happened. Even for Clint, it seemed like a dream. And yet, he knew that it had happened just the way that he remembered it. He could tell it had happened just by studying the silent faces of the other men as they ate their breakfast of biscuits and salted beef.

FIFTEEN

They never did find Doran's camp. Clint could still picture the bounty hunter's horse standing hobbled in a clearing waiting to die.

Even someone like Doran deserved better than an unmarked grave in the hills. The men, quiet at their work in digging the grave and filling it with the body and then dirt, had not even paused long enough to say a few words to send the bounty hunter on his way.

These things, however, seemed lost on Kendal, Witt, and DeGraw.

"What was it like?" Kendal asked Witt a few miles down the trail.

"What was what like?" the youth answered grimly, his newfound seriousness a youthful act.

"Killing a man," Kendal whispered. "What did it feel like?"

Witt pretended to give it some thought. "I can't properly say it felt like anything," he answered at last. Then he joked, "I expect it felt a lot worse for him than it did for me."

"I expect so," Kendal said.

"I got to hand it to you, that was a handy piece of work you did back there," DeGraw said. "Mighty handy piece of work on that bastard."

Witt nodded. "It was something I didn't see a choice about," he answered. "I wasn't left with no choice at all in the matter."

"I can't see where you were," DeGraw said. "Don't you think he would have done the same for us? Hell, men like that, they don't think about nothing but the reward. They ain't like us. They ain't what you could call 'gentlemanly.' Hell, they don't even know what it means."

"Don't think I don't know that," Witt said. "He would have stolen our reward and not thought twice about it."

Listening to Kendal and Witt discussing the killing, it sounded to Clint as if they were discussing their first woman. It was obvious that Witt had gained some measure of dubious respect from the banker's son.

Clint had seen this kind of respect before. It was earned cheaply and didn't last. The kind of respect lauded on men in saloons. Yet, there was a type of man, ignorant and vain, who craved it. And when men started to crave and pursue it, they usually ended badly.

"The main thing is, you can't hesitate," Witt said. "Just gotta pretend they're cans or bottles in some field. Gotta do that, 'cause you can bet your last dollar he's doing the same to you."

"I can understand that," Kendal said seriously. "That makes sense."

Clint had no doubt that it was Witt's age, rather than his gunfighting ability, that had saved him. Doran wasn't a good man, not by any stretch of the word, but he wasn't a killer of boys.

"What do you figure to do with him?" the sheriff asked, whispering alongside Clint.

"I'm not the law, Sheriff," Clint replied.

"Nobody knows what went on back there," the lawman said. "Not for sure."

"I've got a pretty good idea," Clint said. "You want to hear my thinking on it?"

"I ain't particularly interested," the sheriff answered. "You weren't there any more than I was. And I ain't prepared to guess. Not when a boy's life is involved."

"So, you do nothing? That's the way you're going to play this hand?"

"Not nothing. I'll make a full report once I get back," the lawman offered. "But I don't see it starting up some big trial. I don't see that at all. I'll write what I saw and give it to the judge."

Clint stayed silent.

"Hell, Doran was a drifter," the sheriff said. "Scum, if you ask me. Lord knows how many men he shot in cold blood. Bounty hunter is a cousin to the killer, sometimes closer than that. I seen my share of them, believe me on that."

"Want to know what I think?"

"Tell me, you're gonna say it anyway."

"It doesn't matter if I believe you or don't believe you," Clint answered. "The thing is, do you believe yourself? And you have to ask yourself if you want that boy going back to town after this. He's feeling like the last stallion in the world right now. And that's not likely to change anytime soon, if you understand what I'm saying."

The sheriff stayed quiet for a long time, thinking. It was a tough choice, any way you looked at it. It might already be too late, what with the bounty hunter dead and buried in a spot even Clint would probably not be able to find again.

"Let me tell you, only once, I don't need you, Adams," the lawman said. "I don't need you a damn bit to sit and judge me. You ain't nobody to judge me."

"I didn't say I was," Clint replied, then spurred his horse up the trail in order to get away from the sheriff and the rest of them.

He was still moving quickly when the trail became mud as a small stream cut across it. It wasn't much of a stream, maybe three feet wide and a few inches deep. It was a small stream, fed by a spring in the rock outcropping on the trail's left side. Probably only existed when the winter snows melted, like now. And even now, it wasn't much, but it was enough. On the other side of the stream were fresh tracks, the mud kicked up not even dried yet.

Clint pulled up the horse and studied the tracks. Two riders moving quickly. It was only by sheer luck that both horses managed to step into the stream a few feet apart, otherwise he might have mistaken the

THE POSSE FROM ELSINORE

tracks for a single horse or not noticed the tracks at all.

He was out of the saddle, hunching down, studying the tracks when the others arrived.

"What you got there, Adams?" the sheriff said.

"It could be them," Clint said.

The sheriff climbed down and studied the tracks up close. "They're moving fast. If it was them, then they were camped out close to us last night," he said. "Probably up at dawn. We might have caught them if we weren't so busy burying Doran."

"Damn, I could have shot them," Witt said.

Clint knew that the more likely outcome of Witt meeting the outlaws would have been Witt dying. Clint didn't know much about these men, but he knew enough to know that they wouldn't have let Witt sneak up on them while they were relieving themselves, and that, unlike Doran, they wouldn't have hesitated a heartbeat before shooting the boy.

"What do you think, Sheriff?" Clint asked.

"Couple of hours, maybe less," the lawman answered, coming up out of the squat he'd assumed in front of the tracks.

"Close enough to hear the shot," Clint said. "Probably spooked them."

"Maybe," the sheriff answered, his voice becoming distant with some other thought.

"Well, let's not dally here then," DeGraw said. "We move fast, we can catch them."

"And then what, Mr. DeGraw?" the sheriff said. "We catch up to them, we run the risk of them hearing us or seeing us first, then laying a trap ahead. Or maybe you just want to shoot it out on this trail here?"

"He's right, damn, he's right," Kendal said unnecessarily.

"What do you figure, then?" Clint asked. "Track 'em till dark?"

"I'm thinking that maybe we close some miles between them and us," he said. "Get to where we can track them. Maybe surprise 'em in their sleep or catch 'em in the next town."

"I'm thinking that maybe they aren't heading to Reno," Clint said. "Virginia City, Carson City maybe."

"I know," the lawman replied. "This trail, it splits off ahead. If they double back, try to make Utah, maybe San Francisco, we've lost them. I think they're going to be heading somewhere to spend the money."

They climbed back into the saddles and continued on. They rode quickly, at a fast gait, but strung themselves out, just in case they did ride into a trap. The men kept thirty yards between them. If there was an ambush, the two outlaws would only be able to get one or two of them at best before the others could take cover.

The sheriff led the way, then Clint, then Kendal, then DeGraw, with Witt bringing up the rear.

In less than two hours they picked up fresh tracks. They were getting close and they all knew it. Kendal kept his hand on the handle of his pistol. Witt stopped talking. Clint, for his part, was aware of every sound, every leaf and tree on either side of the trail.

They continued on like that for some time, each

man expecting a bullet to find him from some unseen gunman at any moment. Even the horses felt the mood and walked skittishly, their ears pricked up.

At dusk, the sheriff pulled up on the reins where the trail took a gentle turn, then raised his hand for the others to stop. He sat stock-still in the saddle for a spell, then motioned for the others to come forward.

Clint rode up next to him and saw what he saw. The trail divided, with one side heading into open country and the other heading into a rocky ride upward.

"Look there," the lawman said, motioning to the ground.

Clint looked. Two sets of prints marred the ground in a confusion as if the two horses had suddenly become twenty. They filled the entire width of the trail just before the fork.

"Looks like maybe they had a hard time making up their minds," Clint said. "Argued over it. Probably took some time doing it, too."

The lawman nodded. "The one on the left there, see that? He turned, went down that way, then came back."

"Looks like they had themselves a regular party here, don't it?" Witt said, looking down at the tracks.

"They went up that way," DeGraw said, pointing.

"I know where they went," the sheriff snapped. "I'm thinking about why."

"That's heading east, isn't it?" Kendal asked.

"That's right," the sheriff said.

"Then let's get 'em," Witt put in, and he pointed his horse up the trail. "It don't matter to me where we find the sons of bitches. I'll track 'em to Kansas if we have to. Let's get us going. The quicker we catch up to them, the quicker we get the money."

"What's down that way, Sheriff?" Clint asked, indicating the open country.

"It's the way to Reno and Carson City," he said. "Trail back up into the hills."

"So, they're heading east?" Clint said.

"They're heading east," the lawman answered. "Now, you mind telling me why?"

" 'Cause they're looking to get away," Witt said, calling to them, then pointing his horse back. "That's just what they're doing, too."

Clint couldn't help noticing that the young man was following the exact motions that one of the outlaws must have made, heading down the trail and returning before going back down the trail.

There was the chance that the outlaws had spotted them and were leading the men into a trap. But if it was a trap, it was a mighty strange one, being out in the open. Better to box them in or find a higher position up in the hills and shoot down on the men.

Then it came to Clint in a flash. Both men, their pockets filled with gold from the assay office, reached a fork in the road. Their choice was either to head somewhere they could spend the money or to head somewhere they couldn't spend money. A man with money in his pocket to spend doesn't head to town for only one reason—because he's after more money.

"Sheriff, is there a stage that cuts across down there?" Clint asked.

SIXTEEN

They rode quickly then, wanting to gain on the outlaws before dark. If night caught up with them too far from the gunmen, they would lose even more time the next day.

The sheriff wasn't certain when the stage came through the area, but he was fairly sure it was midmorning, perhaps even as late as early afternoon. It would leave Candelaria at dawn the next day and ride hard until it reached Carson City by that evening.

Returning to Candelaria wasn't an option for the posse. The law there would be certain not to listen to the posse's warnings. But even as he rode, Clint knew down in his gut he was right about the stage. Why else would they turn off the trail in a new direction? Even the fact that the outlaws had kept close to ground in town for a full day could be explained by their wanting to get the stage schedule.

After a few miles the open country of high grass became rocky again with the trail narrowing down into a dry streambed where the trail of small stones made it all but impossible to track the outlaws. They followed the stream for a few miles, then reached a hill that was mostly stone and a few pines.

"It's over this hill," the sheriff said, pointing his horse up a narrow path. "There's a road that cuts through direct to Carson City."

The path led up a narrow trail of scrub and stones, then turned into a wider path that ran along the hill. From the crest of the hill Clint could look down the slope at the stage trail, a wide trail of nicely packed earth. For a moment he thought maybe he was wrong. Carson City could be their destination, after all. But no outlaw would add a half day or more to a ride where there was liquor and women to be had at the end of the trail.

The sheriff and Clint saw it at the same time. "They're here," Clint said in whisper. "Somewhere on the hill. If they're going after that stage, they'll do it from this hill. I'd swear to it."

The sheriff nodded, his eyes scanning the hill. They were facing west, the sun spreading the last red across the sky before dark. "That's the way I'd do it," he said. "If it was me, I'd sure as hell do it from here."

Clint stepped down off his horse and the sheriff followed suit. "Witt, take the horses down the hill a ways and find a place to hobble them for the night," Clint said. "Not too far now."

THE POSSE FROM ELSINORE

The boy did as he was told, though he didn't seem all that happy about the chore.

"No fire tonight, boys," the sheriff said, hunching down low to the ground, his eyes still studying the hill, north and south, for any signs of the outlaws. He didn't see anything and neither did Clint. But that didn't mean anything. There was enough cover to hide a herd, and nobody either up or down the hill would see a thing.

"Sheriff, you think they'll make their move on that stage?" DeGraw asked.

"They sure as hell couldn't have picked a better place, now, could they?" the lawman answered.

They ate their supper cold without speaking. The night air could play some funny tricks in the hills where they opened into wide spaces. A voice could carry a mile or more in the quiet, and none of the men wanted to risk even a whisper.

When it was full dark, they put a man standing guard. The sheriff took the first shift, then Kendal, DeGraw, Witt, and Clint.

With the sky turning robin's egg-blue, Clint rose from his bedroll and stood his watch. For a brief moment he thought he saw a flame, the flare of a match further down the hill, then it vanished.

A little before it could properly be called day, except by an Iowa farmer, the rest of the men stirred, then rose from their bedrolls.

They still did not risk speaking, but rather ate their breakfast of stale biscuits without coffee. It could be a long day and all of them knew it. If they were wrong they had lost precious time that could never be made up.

A few hours after dawn, they brought the horses up to just below the crest. A narrow trail led almost vertically down to the main road where the coach would pass. At the first sign of trouble, they would ride down and intervene. The outlaws would not be expecting more men and would be taken by surprise. But the trail leading down was a treacherous one. If they didn't lose a horse on it rushing down, it would be a miracle.

It wasn't until nearly noon, with Witt and Kendal beginning to become anxious, that they heard the distant thunder of the stage, the sound of the approaching Wells Fargo coach and its six-horse team rattling in the hot, motionless air.

"This is it," the sheriff said, mounting his horse.

Clint took his saddle as did the others.

As the stage grew closer, they all held their breath. Suddenly, it was in view, coming smartly around a turn. When the stage was just below them, Clint let his breath out, certain they had been wrong.

"Damn," Witt said.

But no sooner were the words out of the boy's mouth than a shot echoed up from the trail and the sound of the coach ceased.

Clint didn't wait for the sheriff; he spurred his horse furiously, sending it down the steep incline. For fifty yards it was like riding toward the ground, then the trail leveled off some and he could see the bandits just around a second bend.

Both of them were wearing flour sacks with eyes

cut out over their heads, but there was no mistaking that they were the same men from Candelaria and Elsinore.

Clint pulled his Colt from the holster and rode hard down the last patch of trail onto the road. Behind him he could hear the others coming.

As he approached the stage, he could see both rider and shotgun at the top, their hands up over their heads. Off to the side of the stage were two men in suits, hands also high.

The outlaws both had their guns drawn, pointing and motioning.

"Hold it! Hold it right there!" Clint barked as he rode up on the stage.

Clint was maybe fifty yards off, but as soon as the outlaws saw him they started shooting. Both shots missed easily, but the noise spooked the team, which burst forward, nearly knocking the driver and shotgun from their perches on top of the coach.

Then one of the outlaws grabbed out, catching a piece of harness, and quieted the team. The other moved to the side of the road and started firing again.

With shots flying to the left and right of him, Clint's horse panicked and started to pinwheel before Clint could bring him back under control. Still moving, he used the back of the stage as cover as he advanced.

The others passed Clint then retreated, bunching together some as the outlaw kept firing.

Just then, Clint saw the shotgun rider make a move, coming forward on the top of the stage. The outlaw holding the team's harness spotted him and fired, the shot knocking him backward off the rear of the coach.

"Damn it," Sheriff Smith said, then pointed his horse to the left of the stage and started firing at the shotgun rider's killer.

With the sheriff's first shot, both passengers vanished, running up into the hills for cover.

Now, as if for the first time, the outlaws got a look at the posse. Five men against their two. The outlaw holding the harness released it and went for a Winchester in his saddle boot. With the first shot from the rifle, the team bolted again. This time the driver held on as the stage vanished around the bend, leaving the outlaws out in the open.

Clint spurred his horse forward, passing the others as he began firing.

With no stage, no cover, and outnumbered, the outlaws turned and ran.

Clint was moving quickly but pulled up when he saw the road turn down a slight incline. At that moment he caught a flash of Kendal as the youth galloped by, one of those fancy side arms up. The young man might have said something, but Clint couldn't make out the words.

Two shots sounded and then there was the crash of splintering wood and cries of horses. A second later, there was another shot and another crash.

Clint turned the corner in a gallop and immediately pulled up on the reins to a stop. What he saw ahead in the road he hoped he'd never see again.

The driver had been unable to bring the team to a stop. Turning, the wagon had become unbalanced and flipped, the momentum forcing the coach into a small ravine at the side of the road and dragging half the team down with it. The other horses, still in harness, lay twitching and injured across the remainder of the road. It was the stage horses that Kendal's own horse had collided with to disastrous effect.

Kendal's horse lay a few yards ahead, a bone protruding from the left front leg, its eyes wide with terror and pain.

"Goddamn," the sheriff said, pulling up on the reins to walk the horse into the horror.

Clint rode up on the scene slowly, looking for Kendal. He found him a few yards off to the side of the road, beyond the stage and the team. He'd been thrown twenty feet or more, his brains splashed in a bloody stain across the side of a large table-sized rock.

Clint climbed down from his horse and looked at the boy. He must had hit the rock headfirst across where two of its sides met in a sharp angle. The boy's skull was cleaved down past his eyes.

The air was filled with the sound of injured horses, snorting and whinnying.

"Damn." Clint called, "It's bad over here."

"This one's alive still," the sheriff called back. "The driver's alive."

Clint turned to where the sheriff and Witt were bending toward the injured man just off the road. DeGraw was walking through the carnage, coming toward Clint.

"Naw, he's dead," the sheriff called in a low moan. "Damn it, he's dead."

"How bad?" DeGraw said, coming up on Clint. "That boy alive?"

"Bad as I've seen," Clint said. "And he's deader than hell."

DeGraw stepped by Clint and got a look at the boy. He let out a low whistle. "He's dead, sure as hell," he said, then walked back.

Clint closed the boy's eyes and walked back to where the sheriff and Witt stood. At first he thought Witt might be looking at something, examining some new horror on the ground. But as he got closer he saw the boy was gagging, bringing back up his breakfast of hard biscuit.

"We best clean this mess up some," the sheriff said. "You want to start on those horses, I'll do the others?"

Clint reloaded his gun and walked among the injured animals. One by one he put a bullet in each of the horse's ears, kneeling beside each animal and calming it with a smooth stroke across the neck before pulling the trigger. He emptied the gun on the team, reloaded, then fired a shot into Kendal's horse.

The sheriff, for his part, had brought out a length of rope, and with DeGraw's help was using both their horses to drag the coach off the road.

Witt sat on a rock on the side of the road and viewed the carnage with terror-struck eyes.

"It's bad sometimes," Clint said, approaching the boy. "Just got to deal with it in yourself."

"I ain't scared," Witt said.

"Nobody said you were," Clint answered.

"This ain't much to me," the boy spat back. "Kendal was a good man. I'm gonna miss him. But he died like a man. That counts for something.''

Clint didn't answer the patent lies. Instead, he walked over to the sheriff and DeGraw to help pull the stage's wreckage into the ditch.

SEVENTEEN

"Sheriff, Mr. Adams, look here!" Witt called.

Clint stopped the task and walked over to where Witt and DeGraw were standing at the opposite side of the road. The sheriff followed.

There, smashed against a rock, was the strongbox, its side split open and the cloth bags inside burst, pouring their contents out across the ground. Paper currency and coins were scattered in a wide arc around the rock and into the ditch.

"That sure is a lot of money," DeGraw said. "Hell of a lot of money to be left on its own out on this trail all by itself. Kind of makes you feel sorry for it. Makes a fella want to take it up and give it a home."

"Don't even think about it, DeGraw," the lawman answered. "Don't set your mind to it."

"Damn," Witt said, bending down to look at the

money. "I'd be lying if I told you I ever saw more all in one place. Hell, all together in my life, if you added it up, I haven't seen more. Damn, but that's more money than that shabby store will see in a year. Ten years. Hell, ever."

Clint looked at the smashed box. The coins spilled out in a halo around it, and scattered about was the paper money, heavy with mud. It wasn't lost on Clint that the box bore a weird similarity to the way Kendal's skull had been smashed in.

The money, lying as it was in the dirt, seemed to have been imbued with a life, a power of its own. Perhaps because it seemed free for the taking, far from the grasp of bankers and shopkeepers who counted it out to the penny. There it was, a chaos of money scattered in the dirt, uncounted and seemingly not belonging to anyone.

"How much you figure it to be?" Witt asked, without taking his eyes off it.

"Don't matter," the sheriff replied. "It ain't ours to count or to keep. First chance, we're taking this back to the Wells Fargo office."

"Damn, it's a lot of money, ain't it?" Witt murmured. "It's a hell of a lot."

The sheriff gave Clint a small look that meant don't let those two near the money, then walked back to his horse. When he returned, he was carrying an empty saddlebag.

"Reckon it's time to put it here," he said, opening the saddlebag's flap. Then he grabbed a great handful of coins and paper and began loading it into the saddlebag. He worked quickly, handling the money as if it were no more than stones. By the time he was finished, the saddlebag bulged to breaking with the money. Just the weight of it made the sheriff stoop slightly.

"And you're riding with it, I suppose?" DeGraw said, a hard edge to the question. "That's awful convenient now, isn't it?"

"That's right," the sheriff said. "It's riding behind me. You see any problems with that arrangement?"

The four men froze, DeGraw challenging the sheriff without speaking a word.

"I reckon that will do," DeGraw finally answered, his voice returning to its usual speaking tone. "Yes, sir, I reckon that'll have to do for now."

But the sheriff didn't move. He stood his ground in front of DeGraw. "I like you, DeGraw. I like the way you do things. I don't know exactly, but it's amusing I guess you'd say, in Elsinore. You run an honest house, and Lord knows you keep the peace in it. A lawman appreciates that. It's what you would call good citizenship."

"What's your point, Sheriff?" DeGraw asked, holding his ground. "You telling me all this for a reason or just to be talking?"

"My point is, we ain't in Elsinore now," the sheriff said. "Myself, I like you. So what I'm telling you I don't want you to take personal, but I'd no more let you carry this than let you marry my daughter, if I had one. I like you fine, but you so much as move a little finger in the direction of this money, I'll kill you. Nothing personal, but I'd do it in a heartbeat. Do you understand that?"

Oddly, DeGraw smiled. It was a warm, friendly smile. "Sheriff, I wouldn't expect less," he said, still smiling. "Not from you, being an honest man and all. Matter of fact, makes me feel good knowing I know an honest lawman."

"You keep that in mind then," the sheriff said. "Think on it hard. Because being honest I wouldn't lie to you, not about liking you personally and not about killing you if you tried to steal."

They used bedrolls for the dead, covering the bodies in blankets and tying them across the backs of the horses. The stage's passengers had not returned. No one had seen them since the robbery.

"What about those fellas we saw?" Witt asked.

"I saw them run, they're probably still running," the sheriff said.

"We can't just leave them up there," Witt added. "They could be lost up there, for all we know."

"It's a day's walk to Carson City from here," the lawman said. "They have any sense at all, they'll climb back down from the hills and start walking. I can't wait on them."

It was near dusk by the time they began riding again. None of them spoke. The sheriff, thinking about the gold riding behind him, and the others very much aware they were riding in front of dead men.

An hour after they had climbed back into their saddles, the trail narrowed again and the trees thinned out as the hillside became rocky.

"I don't like this, Sheriff," Clint said, slowing his horse a little.

The sheriff nodded in agreement.

"What's that?" Witt asked, riding up beside Clint and the sheriff. "What's that you said?"

It was then that Clint heard the first shot and felt the slug pound into the dead body behind him. His horse panicked, trying to run.

Two more shots rang out, kicking up dirt near DeGraw and the sheriff. Both men cursing, trying to control their horses, pointed them toward the trees.

Witt drew his gun and fired back blindly as more shots came from the rocky slope to their left.

Clint reined in his horse and followed into the trees.

"It's them, damn, it's them," Witt cried as more shots chipped at the trees.

When they were certain that they had cover, the men stopped a little way up the slope.

"Damn it, I knew it," the sheriff said. "They ain't gonna give up on this money."

"You see anything?" DeGraw asked, his gun out, eyes scanning the trees around them in a panic.

"About halfway up, there's a little cutout, two stones," Clint answered. "In there."

"Damn, we got them now," Witt said.

"We got nothin'," the sheriff spat back. "They got the high ground and we got nothin'."

"Can we come up behind them?" DeGraw asked.

"I don't think so," Clint replied. "There's a drop of twenty feet maybe, behind those stones. It's like they put themselves in a little room up there."

"We got to do something," Witt said. "Damn, we got to do something."

Then a voice shouted from the rocks above. "You

down there, bring out the money," the outlaw called.

Clint climbed down off his horse, handed the reins to DeGraw, and moved cautiously forward using the trees for cover. A shot rang out, knocking a patch of bark from the tree Clint stood behind.

"See him?" the sheriff asked.

"He's got a rifle up there," Clint said, watching the powder smoke rise from between the two large stones.

"You hear us down there?" the voice shouted.

"We hear you," the sheriff shouted back as Clint moved closer, dodging behind another tree.

"Bring out that money," came the reply. "Give it to the boy to bring and we'll let you live."

"Go to hell!" the sheriff called back. "Just go to hell, directly."

Three more shots exploded from the rocks, one aimed directly at Clint, the other shots chipping at trees where the others took cover.

"I say we charge them," Witt suggested. "Two of them and four of us. We can take them bastards, easy."

Clint crawled back to where the others waited, just in time to hear the boy's suggestion.

"Charge them with what?" DeGraw answered. "I don't intend to die over Wells Fargo money."

"He's right," the sheriff added. "Got a man up there with a repeater. He'd cut us all down before we got across the trail."

"You want to die for that money?" the outlaw called. "That ain't even your money!"

"He's right," DeGraw replied to no one in particular. "I don't intend to die for some stranger's money. Not like this."

"We can go back," the sheriff said. "Circle up through the trees and head back. You got any ideas, Adams? Now's the time to hear them."

Clint thought about it. The way ahead was blocked, even through the trees. The horses wouldn't make the climb around. The only way, clear way, was to climb as far up as they could make it, using the trees for cover, then head back.

"I ain't running from the likes of them," Witt said. "Not likely."

Clint looked up, letting his eyes rest on a patch of evening sky as it appeared through the trees. It would be dark in an hour and they could wait them out until tomorrow, but they'd be in the same place. Then an idea struck him.

"Sheriff, can you climb a tree?" he asked, still staring up.

Twenty minutes later, the sheriff was fifty feet up in a large pine directly across from the outlaws. Clint hoisted the saddlebag filled mostly with stones and a few coins on his shoulder.

"We're coming out!" DeGraw called as Clint began walking toward the trail.

"Bring it here," the outlaw called from the rocks. "Bring her here!"

Clint took a step out on the trail, expecting to feel a bullet from that repeater smash into his skull and scatter his brains at any moment.

"That's good, good," the outlaw called. "Now, let's see the money."

Clint opened the saddlebag and dug his hand in, pulling out a handful of coins and letting them drop slowly through his fingers back into the bag.

"Good, now put her down!" the outlaw called.

Clint kept walking toward the rocks.

"I said, put her down!"

Clint kept walking, inching his way across the trail.

A gunshot exploded from the rocks and pitched up a portion of dirt so close to his boot it hit his pant leg.

Immediately after the gunman's shot, the sheriff fired the big Sharps into the rocks. His shot was answered by a vicious volley.

Clint dove forward toward the base of the rocky hill, taking shelter between two large stones. Even as he was moving, he listened for the shots from the rocks. Two guns were firing. The sheriff had missed the man with the repeater.

Then there were more shots from the trees. The bullets pounded into the stones, some of them ten feet or less above Clint's head.

The plan had failed. Clint knew it immediately. What he didn't know was how to recross the trail and get back up into those trees.

EIGHTEEN

"They got him!" Witt called. "They killed the sheriff!"

Clint, hunching down in the rocks, could picture it. The sheriff's huge bulk crashing down fifty feet or more through the branches to the ground. The sheriff had missed the first shot. It was his only shot. The outlaw with the repeater would have had time to aim in on the lawman after that first shot. It wouldn't have taken long, a second is all. The lawman was a big target and the tree didn't offer much cover.

"I need help here!" Clint called to Witt and DeGraw. "They got me boxed in."

"Ain't no helping you," the outlaw answered. "No help for you at all. Now just drop that saddlebag and walk right back to your friends."

Clint ignored the advice. The second he set foot on

the trail, coming out into the open, they would cut him down without a second thought.

"At three," DeGraw cried back. "You start on three and keeping going."

"One!" Clint shouted. "Two! Three!" Even before the last number was out of his mouth, Witt and DeGraw started firing at the rocks, their shots landing to the left and right of the small slot the outlaw with the Winchester occupied.

Clint rose up and started running across the road. It was maybe four strides, but it was the longest four strides of Clint's life. Then, too, beyond the road he had maybe fifteen yards before the protection of the first tree.

As he ran, Clint counted shots from the two men. Twelve shots was all he had before they needed to pause and reload. Twelve shots before that bastard with the repeater would put him in the rifle's sights and start squeezing the trigger.

Clint ran low to the ground. Zigzagging his way across the road, he pulled his gun and thumbed back the hammer. As his foot stepped off the trail, he heard the last of the dozen shots roar from the trees. Turning, he spun on his heels and let go with three more shots of his own toward the rocks, firing and running backward at the same time.

Ten yards now, he reckoned, and turned again, running flat out for the trees.

Two shots from the repeater sounded from the rocks, and he felt the air burn with the hot lead near his left ear, the powerful slug parting the air at the side of his head. Then a third shot slammed into his boot's underslung heel, lifting his foot up in midstride and sending him rolling to the ground as a fourth bullet kicked up a spike of dirt not six inches from his head.

The fall left him only a few yards from the cover of the first tree. He turned, rolling on his back, and let go with three more rounds, the bullets chipping rock a few inches from the narrow slot between the stones that protected the outlaw.

Clint fired again and his gun clicked down on a spent cartridge. He cursed and turned, smoothly holstering the pistol and seeing the trees, only yards away, look as distant as China.

Clint rose to a half-stooped position and started moving again, expecting to feel the hot lead pound into his back or explode his skull at any moment. Keeping low, using his hands for purchase on the rocky ground, he made the safety of the tree as another slug ripped into the bark a few inches from his head.

"You made it all right?" DeGraw called. "I'll be damned if you didn't make it."

"Made it," Clint shouted back, his breath coming in ragged bursts. "I need some more cover down here. DeGraw! Witt! You there?"

"Might as well come the rest of the way," DeGraw cried, and began shooting toward the rocks again. He shot rapidly, one shot after another, shooting as fast as he could pull the trigger.

Clint gathered himself up and ran toward the next tree. Still counting shots, he had reached cover before the two men had reached ten.

"Well, hot damn, that was something," Witt said, opening the cylinder and pulling spent shells. "That was purely something special."

Clint, breathing hard now, could only look at the lad.

"And you brought the bag back with you, too," DeGraw said, smiling. "I'll be damned if you ain't the genuine article."

It was true, Clint hadn't even noticed while he was running, but the saddlebag was drapped over his shoulder. Twenty pounds of stones and a handful of gold had almost cost him his life. If he had thought about it at all when he was crouching down there at the base of the rocks, he would have left the damned bag.

A few feet away, the sheriff lay on his back, his head twisted oddly and sitting unnaturally close to his shoulders. Between his eyes, just at the start of the nose, was a single bullet hole. A thin trickle of blood, like a tear, had run down to his mouth and dried.

"Yeah, they got him," DeGraw said. "Got him before he could get that second shot off."

"He was up there talking to himself," Witt said, his voice breathless. "Heard him muttering like a crazy person, saying, 'Shoot, shoot, shoot damn it.' Next thing I know, they shot him. It was like he was talking to them, asking them to shoot him. Crazy thing. He went crazy up there or something. And damn if he didn't fall down the tree head coming first. Right down, like a fence post."

"Strangest thing I've seen in a while," DeGraw

said. "And in my line, I've seen some strange things."

Clint knew what had happened. After that first shot, the sheriff did have the outlaw in his vernier sights. The lawman just couldn't bring himself to pull the trigger. Maybe it was the sight of the man's face hovering in the steel contraption that did it to him. It wasn't the outlaw he was telling to shoot, he was telling himself. Like he was arguing with himself over whether to kill a man he knew would surely kill him.

The sheriff's hesitation couldn't have been more than a second or two. No more time than it took for the outlaw to raise the repeater and find the target in the tree. Yet that was enough.

"He was a decent man," Clint said. "A decent sort of lawman. Fair. They're getting harder and harder to find these days."

"You could say they're dying out," DeGraw said. "A bullet don't care nothing about fair."

Witt looked down at the sheriff's body as if seeing it for the first time. With the heat of the gunfire drained out of him, the reality of the lawman's death was beginning to set in. "I known him my whole life, just about," Witt said. "When I was a little one, even."

"We ain't done with you yet," an outlaw called from across the trail. "We ain't done with none of you bastards yet by a long ways."

"What do you reckon is up across that way?" Clint asked, reloading his Colt. "They got any way to go on us if they took a mind to?"

"Same as this," DeGraw said. "Hill that horses

can't make. If they're leaving, then they're walking. But they ain't leaving. I'd bet on that. They're staying until they get this gold or get dead."

"They can't leave on the trail, neither," Witt added. "They can't get far enough down the trail with the horses to run. Least we can do that."

"We're not running," Clint answered. "Nobody is going anywhere until this is settled."

Just then, a stick came flying over the rocks. It was followed by another, then another.

"What the hell they doing?" DeGraw asked. "They run out of bullets and throwing sticks at us?"

"Not likely," Clint answered. "Not likely at all, but damned if I do know."

"Well, I ain't going down there to find out," Witt said. "My momma didn't raise a fool."

The men watched as deadfall branches continued to fly up out of the rocks to land in the middle of the trail. One of the outlaws must have been working up in the rocks, collecting every piece of wood he could lay hands on. Clint could only guess at how far back he was working. But he must have been going a sizable distance to gather that much wood.

"You ever see anything like this?" Clint asked, watching as more branches flew from the rocks, some of them quite large, some as small as kindling and others as long and thick as a man's arm.

Whatever the outlaws were, they weren't lazy. The branches and sticks continued flying at a steady pace for a good hour. Soon the trail was jammed with them for five yards in either direction.

Dusk faded slowly into a thickening darkness and

the wood continued to fly down onto the trail. It came less quickly now, but it sailed over the rocks steadily.

Then, when it was almost full dark, the activity stopped.

"Guess they got tired," Witt said, smiling. "Foolish thing to do, anyways."

"What the hell are they up to?" DeGraw said, squinting down at the long jumble of wood.

Then there was something else, a glint of metal in the moonlight, and something hit the pile.

"Now what was that?" Clint asked.

But before either of the other two men could even think to answer, a light flared in the rocks, casting a weird orange glow across the rocks.

The light faded, then flew up over the rocks. Clint saw now, the light was a torch. It hung in the air briefly before coming down in the center of the trail. It hit the sticks and Clint knew. The glint was the pint kerosene can the outlaws threw down into the wood.

The fire flared and spread, eventually covering the entire length of the woodpile.

"Those boys have gone and built themselves a fire," Clint said.

"Damn stupid thing to do," Witt said. "Now we can see them if they try and sneak down on us."

"And they can see us," Clint said. "They ain't going to go anywhere without that money. It seems that they've made up their minds on that."

"They can't keep it going all night," Witt said. "There ain't enough wood up there to keep it going all night, I'll tell you that for sure."

"I don't know, they just might try," DeGraw said.

"They seem determined, if I do say so myself."

Clint watched the fire burn, lighting the rocks and the tree line with orange flame. At the center of the trail it was nearly bright as day.

It was full dark and the outlaws showed no signs of quitting the fire. Every few minutes another branch would fly over the rocks to land in the middle of the blaze, sending up a stream of sparks into the night sky.

"They are, they're gonna keep at it all night," Witt said. "Them bastards."

"We sleep in shifts tonight," Clint said. "Witt, you sleep first, then me, and then DeGraw. Two men awake and one asleep. Only way to do it."

"Anyway you look at it, it's gonna be a hell of a night," DeGraw said, his eyes fastened on the fire. "I can't see no way out and they sure as hell can't see no way in."

"It doesn't make sense," Clint said, studying the flames. "Just doesn't make any sense at all."

"It don't make sense, but there it is," Witt answered.

Clint watched as the boy took a position against a tree and tilted his hat down to sleep.

Then Clint hunched down and watched the fire. The flames, which were already starting to die down, cast flickering orange shadows on the rocks, turning the small space into something that looked very much like hell itself.

NINETEEN

"There's three of us now, Adams," DeGraw said, hunkering down next to Clint as they watched the fire. "Two and a half, if you know what I mean."

"I know what you mean," Clint said. "I'm just not too sure I know what you're getting at."

DeGraw turned to face Clint. "I'm a businessman, pure and simple," he said. "And I'm not ashamed to say it, I'm successful at it. Business is about risk. You take a big risk, you better be damned sure there's a big reward. Big risk like spending your life digging in the dirt and hoping that the gold is where you're digging. That's a big risk. Never cared for those."

"You're talking, but not saying much," Clint answered, not taking his eyes off the burning trail.

"I'm leading up to it, listen to me," DeGraw said, his voice urgent and confidential at the same time.

"Myself, I don't take big risks. If I make a thousand dollars I'll do it a hundred dollars at a time. Better odds that way. You understand what I'm getting at?"

"Keep talking," Clint said.

"When we started out on this little enterprise, there were five of us," DeGraw said. "Five of us against two. Those are the kind of odds I like."

"And now that we're three, you don't like the odds anymore?"

"Exactly," DeGraw answered. "And you got to figure those ole boys across there, well, they sure as hell know what they're about. Right now, right this minute, they're being better businessmen. Big risk and big reward. Don't think they don't understand that."

"And we're what?"

"Big risk, little reward," DeGraw said. "Hell, there's the five thousand from the reward money and maybe a little more, seeing they killed two more Wells Fargo men. But the company don't give a damn about the men. Let's say they decide to put up another thousand dollars in reward money."

"And?"

"And nothing. What I'm saying is that we're out here, the three of us, getting shot at and sticks thrown at us for two thousand apiece? I don't like those odds, Adams, not one little bit."

"And those dead men? Don't they mean anything to you?" Clint asked, turning to face DeGraw for the first time.

"They're dead," DeGraw answered smoothly. "Nothing we do is going to bring them back. They'd be just as dead if those fellas shot them or if they fell down a well."

"After what you've seen, just today, you can sit there and tell me it doesn't make any difference if those boys pay?" Clint asked. "In case you forgot, we've got ourselves four bodies back there by the horses. More bodies back in Elsinore. None of that means anything to you?"

DeGraw seemed to think about it. From the look on his face, Clint knew he wasn't reconsidering anything, just figuring a way to explain himself. "What it means to me is that they're dead and they're gonna keep on being dead till kingdom come," DeGraw said. "That's just the way it is. Nothing changes that. Nothing we do here is gonna change that. I'm alive and you're alive. Now we can make the best of it or act like damned fools and risk dying for money that we ain't got a chance in hell of keeping."

"What's making the best of it?" Clint asked. "What's that mean?"

"Means that we divide the money here and now," DeGraw answered. "We split it two ways and start walking. You walk north and I'll head south. Up over the hill tonight and start on our seperate ways."

"What about the boy?" Clint asked. DeGraw had made no mention of him. Indeed, he'd suggested a two-way division of the money. "You just planning on leaving the boy here with the bodies at his back and those bastards in front of him?"

"I don't like to say it, but that's the way it's gotta be," DeGraw said. "We leave him here to shoot it out with them. I figure he'll last a day, maybe more.

That's plenty of time to get a lead on them. That day of walking gets us to a rail or a town with enough money to go anywhere."

Clint looked away from DeGraw, then back again. "Listen to me, because I'm only going to explain this once," he said. "You mention that plan again, and I'll kill you. Right here. Mention it to the boy, and I'll kill you. Make a move alone with all the money for yourself, I'll kill you. You think a day's ride is gonna keep me from shooting you down like vermin, then you are pitifully mistaken."

"You're a fool, Adams," DeGraw said. "Nothing but a damned fool. I'm offering you the business proposition of a lifetime and you're talking about shooting me."

"You're offering me nothing," Clint said. "You're offering me a chance to help you out of here with the money. If you thought you could do it yourself, you would. But you're too cowardly to try. First chance after you felt safe enough, you'd double back and put a bullet in me."

DeGraw was silent for a long time. Finally he said, "You're wrong about that. About me being a coward."

Then they fell into silence again. Clint had nothing else to say to him.

After several hours, Clint rose from his position and woke the boy. The young man got to his feet slowly, rubbing the sleep out of his eyes.

The fire had nearly burned out, yet every so often another branch would sail over the rocks.

"Anything happens, you wake me, hear?" Clint said, settling down for a few hours sleep.

"I'll do it," the boy said.

"And do yourself a favor," Clint said. "Don't listen to DeGraw anymore. The way he's talking is likely to get us all killed. And keep an eye on that money, I no more trust him around it than I'd trust a wolf around a new calf."

The boy nodded to show that he understood, but it was a weak nod. DeGraw's business proposition was still rattling around in his head. Perhaps the boy, too, had some vague plan for making off with the Wells Fargo gold.

Despite himself, Clint fell into a deep sleep almost immediately. But it seemed that he had no sooner shut his eyes than he snapped awake with the feeling that something was wrong.

As Clint awoke he didn't see the boy and didn't see DeGraw. The camp was hushed in the predawn dark.

"Witt, you there?" he whispered and received no answer. "Witt?"

Crawling forward cautiously, he saw that the fire on the trail had burned itself out. Only a few embers glowed at the center. Then, turning from the trail, he looked for the saddlebag of gold and wasn't surprised when he saw it was missing.

The horses were there, though, as was the dead sheriff, that was something.

Drawing his gun, Clint started cautiously through the trees. He had gone about a quarter mile when he heard voices ahead whispering. Two men, talking with great urgency. One of the voices he recognized as DeGraw's, the other wasn't Witt's.

Clint thumbed back the hammer and walked cautiously forward toward the voices. Minding to walk quietly, he moved with deliberate slowness.

"Stranger, what're you sayin'?" one voice asked. "Just what are you sayin'?"

"I'm sayin' there's a piss pot full of gold here, enough for three men to share," DeGraw said. "I'm sayin' fifteen thousand at least. More than enough."

"More if it's only two men doing the counting, ain't it?" the voice, which Clint now recognized as that of the outlaw, answered.

"I'm telling you not to chance it," DeGraw replied. "Your life worth that kind of chance?"

Clint peered out from behind a tree and saw them, both of them, DeGraw and the gunman, maybe fifteen yards apart, each behind his own tree.

"Ain't no big chance at all," the outlaw replied. "Way I see it, we got you trapped. You, that there boy, and that other fella."

"I told you, he's crazy. A mad dog," DeGraw answered. "Hell, I'm scared of him. I tell you he's crazy."

"Friend, I think you're crazy, coming out here like this," the outlaw said. "Just to be talking about it, you got the gold with you?"

Clint looked around his tree, saw the gold at DeGraw's feet.

"I'm talking about a business proposition," DeGraw said. "Both of you seem like reasonable men."

"I'd reasonably kill you rather than keep talking to your kind," the outlaw said. "You sound like a damned banker, the way you talk."

"I'm no banker," DeGraw answered. "I'm just a businessman. What I'm telling you is good business. I'm offering you boys a deal where nobody gets shot or dead. What I'm offering you is fair."

"Why is it every time a banker says 'fair' I feel like reaching for my gun?" the outlaw answered.

DeGraw paused, about to say something, but gunshots rang out from behind him. "What the hell?" he said.

"Hell is right, you damned banker bastard," the outlaw answered. "That's your two friends back there dying."

Clint knew immediately what had happened: While the outlaw had kept DeGraw occupied, the other outlaw had crawled around to ambush the boy.

More shots rang out then. The boy wasn't dead, not yet. Clint ran up, tree to tree with DeGraw.

"You son of a bitch," Clint said, holding a gun to DeGraw's head. "I'm taking the money."

The outlaw a few yards off fired, the bullet drilling into the tree in front of them.

"You crazy? He's shooting at us," DeGraw said.

Keeping his pistol aimed at DeGraw's head, Clint grabbed the saddlebag. "Why don't you just make a deal with him, like a businessman?"

Backing off from the tree, Clint ran back toward the camp. It seemed that with each step he took more shots sounded. As long as he could hear gunshots he knew the boy was still alive.

Finally he saw Witt. The boy was sitting with his back toward a tree, firing without aiming over his shoulder. A large stain of blood blossomed at his stomach.

Clint came in close, firing as he ducked behind a tree near Witt's.

"How you doing there, boy?" he asked as a bullet pounded into the tree in front of him.

"It's bad. Real bad. The bastard gut-shot me," Witt said, his voice tight with pain. "You got the gold?"

"I got it," Clint answered, then leaned around the tree to fire.

There were more shots now, this time from the direction of where DeGraw hunkered behind the tree.

"It was a trap," Witt said.

Clint looked over at the boy. In the pale predawn light, he could see the boy's sweat-soaked face contorted into a mask of pain. "What that bastard tell you?" Clint asked. "What'd DeGraw tell you?"

"Said we'd have a better chance if we surrounded them, go round on each side," Witt said.

Clint saw DeGraw's plan. Send the boy around one side and he'd go round the other. The boy would draw off both outlaws and keep them busy long enough for DeGraw to walk out of there. No doubt, DeGraw intended to leave Clint to the tender mercies of the gunmen. Leave him sleeping there to be murdered without the chance to open his eyes.

"I'm dyin', Mr. Adams," Witt said. "I can feel myself leaking out, like."

"Just sit there, son," Clint said. "Try not to move around. It'll only make it worse."

TWENTY

Clint could see no way out. He didn't know how much more time the boy had to live. It could be an hour or a day. It was hard to tell with a gut-shot wound. Someone who was gut-shot bled as much inside as out.

He'd seen fat men gut-shot who didn't bleed hardly at all. After they were dead, a doctor would make a little cut and the blood would rush out of them, black and clotted, like water from a pump spigot. Other times, it would just leak out of them little by little, until their faces turned pale as flour and their hearts had nothing more to pump.

The only thing that was certain was that the boy was as good as dead. It was only a matter of time.

"It hurts real bad, real bad, Mr. Adams," Witt moaned. "Never had nothing hurt like this before."

Clint leaned around the tree and fired. The outlaw fired back almost immediately. It was nearly the same situation as before, with outlaws and posse facing each other across the trail, except now it was much closer.

Clint leaned to fire again, but before he could pull the trigger, a bullet ripped into the tree above his head. Turning back, he saw the shooter. The outlaw who had been talking to DeGraw had come up behind them. It was the redheaded gunman, Vizard.

"Don't do nothing foolish now," the outlaw said. He had DeGraw caught in the crook of his arm. In the other hand was a pistol aimed at DeGraw's head. "My friend here and me got a little business we want to talk on. Now, we're all gonna talk like gentleman or I'll blow what he got for brains to hell and gone."

"We can all work this out," DeGraw said. "We just got to all calm down and negotiate."

Clint had to hand it to DeGraw, the bastard was as calm as he'd ever seen a man with a gun to his head.

"Listen to your friend here or he dies," Vizard answered.

Clint didn't answer. There was nothing he could say that would stop the outlaw from killing DeGraw. The man was as good as dead.

"What we have here is what you could call a business impasse," DeGraw said. "Pure and simple. But there doesn't have to be no more dying over this thing."

Clint kept his pistol up, wondering if he could shoot around DeGraw's miserable head and hit the outlaw.

"You listening to me, Adams?" DeGraw snapped.

"We got to settle this piece of business now. Don't just sit there like a damned fool."

DeGraw would make a deal with the devil himself, Clint thought. Didn't matter a bit who you put in front of him, he'd try to talk his way into the best deal. For a man like that, a gun to the head wasn't much more than a banker behind a desk.

"Adams, you listen to me!" DeGraw shouted, his voice still calm and in control. "We are dealing with these men here."

Just then, Witt seemed to awaken. He opened his eyes slowly, as if even that act was painful. The boy's face was ghostly pale in the darkness. "You bastard," he said. "You filthy bastard, you killed me."

Clint watched as the boy raised his gun with a shaking hand.

"Don't do it," Vizard said, thumbing back the hammer on his pistol. "Don't do it, boy. I'll shoot him."

"Bastard," Witt said, then fired. "You filthy son of a bitch bastard."

But it wasn't Vizard that the boy was aiming at. The bullet hit its mark dead center over DeGraw's heart.

DeGraw slumped in the outlaw's arm and very nearly dragged the gunman down to the ground before he released him. But even before DeGraw hit the ground, Vizard fired, the bullet shattering Witt's skull and blowing the boy's brains out the back across the tree.

Before the outlaw could turn his gun, Clint fired, hitting the outlaw in the throat, killing him instantly.

"Frank!" the other outlaw called from the trees. "Frank!"

"He's dead," Clint called back, reloading his revolver. "He's dead."

This bit of news was followed by silence. A second later, Clint heard running as the outlaw lit out down the hill. Shouldering the gold, Clint took off after the gunman.

Breaking from the trees, Clint saw a figure hightailing it down the slope of the hill at a full run, the repeater held in one hand. The figure was no more than a shadow really, yet Clint followed.

Even with the weight of the gold on his shoulder, Clint gained on the figure. When the gunman reached the rocks, he turned, bringing the repeater up to his shoulder quickly, and fired. The rifle spit flame and a shot seared by Clint's head.

Clint returned fire with his pistol, only to hear the shot glance off rock.

The gunman turned again and kept running, desperate to reach the shelter of the rocks. Halfway across the road, the outlaw stumbled, falling into the dying fire and sending a short plume of sparks into the air as he cried out with pain.

This was the moment Clint had been waiting for. Holstering his pistol, he ran as fast as he could down the remainder of the hill. As the gunman tried to rise, Clint's boots landed in the remains of the fire. In a flash, he had the gunman around the throat, their feet kicking up the embers and burnt branches around them.

Just when Clint thought he had him, the gunman

came up with the butt of his rifle and landed a dizzying blow across Clint's skull. Clint responded by releasing the man's throat and punching out to connect with the outlaw's jaw. The blow sent the gunman staggering back, his feet tangling in the coals until he finally fell.

Before the man could put another shell in the repeater's chamber, Clint kicked out, knocking the gun from the man's hands. The rifle flew clear of the fire, then Clint reached down and pulled the outlaw up by the front of his shirt.

The man grunted, cursing, and let fly with a blow that Clint easily ducked. Then Clint let go with his own punch, hitting the outlaw solidly on the jaw. The blow knocked his head clean back and sent him staggering across the trail to land against a rock.

"Bastard," the outlaw spat and went for his gun as he took a step forward.

But Clint was faster; the Colt had cleared leather and was leveled before the gunman had raised his gun.

Clint's shot pounded into his chest, knocking him back against the rocks. The outlaw slumped slowly down to the ground, his feet splayed out in front of him.

Clint holstered the gun and stood there studying the dead man. Funny how they always looked less mean with the life blown out of them.

It was almost dawn, the first birds had begun singing, the sky was turning a gray-blue. There was a sharp chill in the air, but no clouds were visible.

Clint noticed the rifle, the repeater, lying a few feet

away. He holstered the Colt, walked the two steps, and picked it up.

When he turned back to the dead man, the outlaw had the pistol raised. A small smile was playing across the gunman's lips. "You a dead man, too. Dead as hell, you son of a bitch," the outlaw gasped and fired.

Clint felt the slug pound into his shoulder even as he drew the Colt and fired back. The gunman slumped forward now, dead for certain with a bullet in his forehead. He sat there with his eyes wide open, a look of mute surprise on his face and a large hole in the center of his forehead.

Clint staggered back with the force of the shot, then straightened up. He stood there for a moment, wondering why he hadn't fallen down or wasn't dead. The bullet had struck directly over his heart. It was then he noticed that the slug had ripped into the saddlebag still slung across his shoulder.

It was a nasty piece of work, any way you chose to look at it. A nasty piece of work, indeed, and nothing to do but do it and move on.

There were bodies to be secured to horses, and a long and lonely ride back to town.

Clint found the outlaws' horses up on the hill behind their camp. The gold from the assay office was hidden under a rock in their camp.

When the bodies were tied down across the saddles and covered as best as was possible, Clint led the horses by a length of rope down the trail. He was a good day's ride from Carson City, and it was midmorning by the time he led the horses with their horrible burdens down the trail.

He pushed the horses hard, moving quickly, not wanting to make camp with just dead men for company.

It was full dark when he spotted the city in the distance with its warm glow of yellow lights burning. He led the string of horses down the center of the street to the sheriff's office. There were a few men out on the boards, and when they saw the horses and what lay slung over the saddles, they followed Clint, not speaking and keeping a respectful distance, to the sheriff's office.

Clint could imagine how he looked to these men. He had ridden out of the night as unexpected as anything these people would hope to see. He was covered in soot from the fire, his face was bruised from the fight, and he'd ridden the entire day leading behind him a string of dead men tied down across saddles.

There were a dozen or more men following when Clint reached the sheriff's office. They stared steadily, their faces questioning, but no words issuing from their mouths. As word spread, more men strolled out of the saloons and hotels. Soon the sidewalk was filled with a loose circle of gawking onlookers.

The lawman, a big man with a think mustache, ambled out the door. There was an amiable look on his face, but then he saw Clint and the horses that trailed behind him.

"What in hell you got there, stranger?" he asked. "What did you bring into my town?"

Clint stepped down from the horse and tied the others to the post. He did not answer, rather he went about the work at hand.

"I'm talking to you," the sheriff said. "What the hell you up to?"

"Got a story to tell you, Sheriff," Clint answered, approaching the sheriff with the saddlebag.

"It better be a damned good one," the lawman said, opening the saddlebag and reaching cautiously inside.

When the sheriff raised his hand it was filled with gold coins.

The men standing in a loose circle let out a small gasp.

"It's a good one," Clint said. "You can count on that much."

"I'm sure I can," the lawman answered as he judged the weight of the saddlebag, then looked toward the dead men tied across the horses.

"I'd appreciate some whiskey," Clint said. "It's been a thirsty day."

The sheriff sent one of the gawkers to the saloon for a bottle, and the two men stepped into the sheriff's office so Clint could tell the story.

The telling of it took most of the night and most of the bottle.

TWENTY-ONE

The town of Elsinore didn't look much different than the first time Clint rode into it. The town wasn't much to look at, but compared to what he'd been looking at over the past few days, it was paradise.

It took three days for the sheriff in Carson City to clear up the mess with Vizard and Montano. Wells Fargo sent a man up from San Francisco to look at the bodies before they went into the ground.

The reward was seven thousand dollars, which the company paid Clint in gold along with a letter from a vice president in San Francisco thanking him for the help.

Now, riding into Elsinore again with seven thousand dollars, he knew how to spend the reward money.

It was May that answered the door to the whorehouse. She seemed surprised to see him, but let him in.

"I suppose you're here to tell me about DeGraw," she said, leading Clint into the parlor. "The Wells Fargo office wired that he was dead."

"They weren't lying," Clint answered.

"I never thought they were," she said. "He was fine, I suppose. Not like some of them."

"I figured I'd give his share of the reward to you," Clint said.

"That man never got any reward," May said. "What are you up to?"

"I figure he was owed something is all."

She laughed at this. "He more than likely got what he was owed," she said.

"More than likely," Clint agreed. "But I'm giving you the money anyway."

She watched, her eyes growing wide, as Clint began piling the gold coins on the table that sat between them. When he was finished, there were ten large piles of coins.

"A lot of money," she said.

"Six thousand," Clint answered.

"That was all of it, wasn't it? All the reward, I mean."

"I kept some," Clint said. "I figured you could use this. Maybe head back East."

She thought about it, then finally shook her head. "I figure I could stay here," she said.

"And do what?"

"Banker's been coming around, asking for money," she answered. "Says that a thousand is still owed on the house. I could pay him back, run this place myself."

Clint nodded. "It sounds like a plan."

"You want a job, Clint?" she asked. "Room and board, and incidentals included. It would be nice to have a man around the house, if you know what I'm getting at."

"I think I'll be riding on," Clint said.

"But not right now?" she said, her lips pouting a little.

"But not right now," he answered.

She led him back to the room and closed the door. "Clint, I was wondering if you could possibly give me some help with this robe?" she asked, untying the front and then letting it drop completely off her shoulders to the floor to gather in a small pile at her feet.

She stood before him naked in the afternoon light, her large breasts rising and falling steadily with her breathing. Her nipples were erect in the cool air.

Clint stepped toward her and gathered the woman up in his arms, then bent to kiss her deeply on the mouth.

He could feel her relax in his arms, pressing her smooth, firm body against his. Reaching down between them, he let his fingers drift lightly over her silken patch and felt that it was wet.

Then gently he gathered her up in his arms and lifted her to the bed. She lay down easily, spreading out before him, stretching her long smooth legs.

"Oh, you've had such a hard time, haven't you?"

she purred. "Well, I'll make it all right. Everything better."

Clint unfastened his gun belt and set it down on the chair, then began working on his shirt. She watched him undress hungrily from the bed, her long slim fingers playing across her nipples, teasing them so that they were even harder.

When he was naked, Clint climbed into the bed and felt her hand reach for his member. She took it gently between her fingers and stroked, letting just her fingertips play up and down the shaft's underside.

Slowly then, she rolled onto her back, pulling him with her. Clint eagerly followed as she spread her legs wide and gently guided his thick, throbbing member into her.

When she released his shaft, the tip was just buried in her. Then she reached up, her eyes smoldering, as she pulled him down by the shoulders. Inch by inch his shaft vanished into her hot, moist womanhood.

Slowly, she brought her hips up off the bed to meet the shaft and drive it deeper within herself. Then, when it was completely buried, she let out a long, low moan.

Clint rested like that for a moment, his shaft inside of her, then slowly, slowly began to pull it out. When just the tip remained again, he pushed it back in with the same teasing slowness.

Soon she was writhing beneath him, her hips moving in a slow, grinding motion as if to urge him even deeper inside.

Cupping one of her breasts in his hand, he bent his head and took the nipple gently between his lips, pulling and toying with it. Then he used his tongue, stroking the thick pink nipple first one way and then the other. She let out a low moan beneath him, and he switched to the other perfumed breast.

Abandoning the breasts, he began moving his member more quickly, using long steady strokes in and out of her as she squirmed and moaned under him.

As he picked up speed, she lifted her legs, locking her slim ankles behind his back and pulling him tightly into her. Her hands came up then and she dug her nails into his shoulders as he continued his long, delicious strokes.

Finally, they reached their end together. She let out a moaning scream as Clint exploded inside of her.

Out in the kitchen, two of the girls sat at the table drinking coffee.

"You hear that?" one of the girls asked.

"Sounded like May, didn't it?" the other replied.

"Sure did. I didn't know she was working this early."

"Neither did I."

"I ain't heard her do it like that since that fella came through."

"That Clint fella?"

"That's the one."

"Honey, from what she told me, he ain't no work at all," came the answer.

Watch for

LADY ON THE RUN

190th novel in the exciting GUNSMITH series
from Jove

Coming in October!

J. R. ROBERTS
THE GUNSMITH

__THE GUNSMITH #163:	THE WILD WOMEN OF GLITTER GULCH	0-515-11656-4/$3.99
__THE GUNSMITH #165:	THE DENVER RIPPER	0-515-11703-X/$3.99
__THE GUNSMITH #170:	THE ELLIOTT BAY MURDERS	0-515-11918-0/$4.50
__THE GUNSMITH #174:	GUNQUICK	0-515-11880-X/$4.99
__THE GUNSMITH #181:	THE CHALLENGE	0-515-11999-7/$4.99
__THE GUNSMITH #182:	WINNING STREAK	0-515-12017-0/$4.99
__THE GUNSMITH #183:	THE FLYING MACHINE	0-515-12032-4/$4.99
__THE GUNSMITH #184:	HOMESTEAD LAW	0-515-12051-0/$4.99
__THE GUNSMITH #185:	THE BILOXI QUEEN	0-515-12071-5/$4.99
__THE GUNSMITH #186:	SIX FOR THE MONEY	0-515-12082-0/$4.99
__THE GUNSMITH #187:	LEGBREAKERS AND HEARTBREAKERS	0-515-12105-3/$4.99
__THE GUNSMITH #188:	THE ORIENT EXPRESS	0-515-12133-9/$4.99
__THE GUNSMITH #189:	THE POSSE FROM ELSINORE	0-515-12145-2/$4.99
__THE GUNSMITH #190:	LADY ON THE RUN (10/97)	0-515-12163-0/$4.99

Payable in U.S. funds. No cash accepted. Postage & handling: $1.75 for one book, 75¢ for each additional. Maximum postage $5.50. Prices, postage and handling charges may change without notice. Visa, Amex, MasterCard call 1-800-788-6262, ext. 1, or fax 1-201-933-2316; refer to ad #206g

Or, check above books   Bill my: ☐ Visa ☐ MasterCard ☐ Amex _____ (expires)
and send this order form to:
The Berkley Publishing Group   Card#_____

P.O. Box 12289, Dept. B   Daytime Phone # _____ ($10 minimum)
Newark, NJ 07101-5289   Signature_____
Please allow 4-6 weeks for delivery.   Or enclosed is my: ☐ check ☐ money order
Foreign and Canadian delivery 8-12 weeks.

Ship to:

Name_____   Book Total $_____
Address_____   Applicable Sales Tax $_____
   (NY, NJ, PA, CA, GST Can.)
City_____   Postage & Handling $_____
State/ZIP_____   Total Amount Due $_____

Bill to: Name_____

Address_____ City_____
State/ZIP_____

First in an all-new series from the creators of Longarm!

BUSHWHACKERS

They were the most brutal gang of cutthroats ever assembled. And during the Civil War, they sought justice outside of the law—paying back every Yankee raid with one of their own. They rode hard, shot straight, and had their way with every willin' woman west of the Mississippi. No man could stop them. No woman could resist them. And no Yankee stood a chance of living when Quantrill's Raiders rode into town...

Win and Joe Coulter become the two most wanted men in the West. And they learn just how sweet—and deadly—revenge could be...

BUSHWHACKERS by B. J. Lanagan
0-515-12102-9/$5.99

BUSHWHACKERS #2: REBEL COUNTY
0-515-12142-8/$4.99

Coming in November 1997: **BUSHWHACKERS #3: THE KILLING EDGE** 0-515-12177-0/$4.99

VISIT THE PUTNAM BERKLEY BOOKSTORE CAFÉ ON THE INTERNET:
http://www.berkley.com

Payable in U.S. funds. No cash accepted. Postage & handling: $1.75 for one book, 75¢ for each additional. Maximum postage $5.50. Prices, postage and handling charges may change without notice. Visa, Amex, MasterCard call 1-800-788-6262, ext. 1, or fax 1-201-933-2316; refer to ad #705

Or, check above books and send this order form to:	Bill my: ☐ Visa ☐ MasterCard ☐ Amex _____ (expires)
The Berkley Publishing Group	Card#_____
P.O. Box 12289, Dept. B	Daytime Phone #_____ ($10 minimum)
Newark, NJ 07101-5289	Signature_____

Please allow 4-6 weeks for delivery. Or enclosed is my: ☐ check ☐ money order
Foreign and Canadian delivery 8-12 weeks.

Ship to:

Name_____	Book Total $_____
Address_____	Applicable Sales Tax $_____ (NY, NJ, PA, CA, GST Can.)
City_____	Postage & Handling $_____
State/ZIP_____	Total Amount Due $_____

Bill to: Name_____

Address_____City_____
State/ZIP_____

A special offer for people who enjoy reading the best Westerns published today.

If you enjoyed this book, subscribe now and get...

TWO FREE WESTERNS

A $7.00 VALUE–NO OBLIGATION

If you would like to read more of the very best, most exciting, adventurous, action-packed Westerns being published today, you'll want to subscribe to True Value's Western Home Subscription Service.

TWO FREE BOOKS

When you subscribe, we'll send you your first month's shipment of the newest and best 6 Westerns for you to preview. With your first shipment, two of these books will be yours as our introductory gift to you absolutely *FREE* (a $7.00 value), regardless of what you decide to do.

Special Subscriber Savings

When you become a True Value subscriber you'll save money several ways. First, all regular monthly selections will be billed at the low subscriber price of just $2.75 each. That's at least a savings of $4.50 each month below the publishers price. Second, there is never any shipping, handling or other hidden charges— *Free home delivery*. What's more there is no minimum number of books you must buy, you may return any selection for full credit and you can cancel your subscription at any time. A TRUE VALUE!

Mail the coupon below

To start your subscription and receive 2 FREE WESTERNS, fill out the coupon below and mail it today. We'll send your first shipment which includes 2 FREE BOOKS as soon as we receive it.

Mail To: **True Value Home Subscription Services, Inc. P.O. Box 5235 120 Brighton Road, Clifton, New Jersey 07015-5235**

YES! I want to start reviewing the very best Westerns being published today. Send me my first shipment of 6 Westerns for me to preview FREE for 10 days. If I decide to keep them, I'll pay for just 4 of the books at the low subscriber price of $2.75 each; a total $11.00 (a $21.00 value). Then each month I'll receive the 6 newest and best Westerns to preview Free for 10 days. If I'm not satisfied I may return them within 10 days and owe nothing. Otherwise I'll be billed at the special low subscriber rate of $2.75 each; a total of $16.50 (at least a $21.00 value) and save $4.50 off the publishers price. There are never any shipping, handling or other hidden charges. I understand I am under no obligation to purchase any number of books and I can cancel my subscription at any time, no questions asked. In any case the 2 FREE books are mine to keep.

Name

Street Address | Apt. No.

City | State | Zip Code

Telephone | Signature

Terms and prices subject to change. Orders subject to acceptance by True Value Home Subscription Services, Inc.

(if under 18 parent or guardian must sign)

12145-2